DUNGEON MASTER

Summer of Adventures #1

Alex Silver

CONTENTS

COPYRIGHT

Cover Design by Alex Silver

ISBN: 978-1-7776786-4-7

BLURB

Slinging coffee is never boring. When a new customer catches my eye, I do what comes natural and flirt with him. To my delight, Martin flirts back. He soon becomes the perfect distraction from my gaming group pressuring me into DMing our next D&D campaign.

Then I overhear Martin designing his dream dungeon, and I just know he's everything I'm looking for in a man. What could be better than a hot summer fling with my very own personal DM? There's just one problem, I should maybe have checked which type of Dungeon Master Martin meant when I asked him to take me on an adventure.

Dungeon Master is a kinky M/M romance with some BDSM elements including: sounding, impact play, and roleplay. It's a spinoff from Table Topped, but it stands alone.

Tags: Low angst, fluff, Bob wants a protector, Bob can rescue himself, flirty barista, meeting at the coffee shop, What type of dungeon master are you? Going on an adventure, Martin is full of surprises.

CHAPTER 1

Bob

I always meet the most interesting people at Sin and Chocolate, the bakery and coffee shop where I work. Slinging coffee and pastries might not be what I dreamed of doing as a child, but I enjoy it nonetheless. Once I make my way into management, I might even be able to start saving for a bigger place than my current crappy studio apartment.

For now, the tips are booming, and I'm on track to train as a supervisor at the end of the summer when my current supervisor plans on moving. Food service is a good fit for me. I enjoy being surrounded by people in most situations. When they aren't over-the-top cantankerous, anyway.

One of my favorite things about working at Sin and Chocolate is that we're an LGBT+ friendly establishment in a progressive city. Vancouver is a gorgeous place to live and I'm into the laid-back vibe here. Several of my coworkers are queer, like me.

Pascal, who bakes most of our in-house pastry offerings, met his boyfriend through answering an ad looking for a roommate on the shop's bulletin board. Most of their friends are regulars, so I've overheard way too much about their love lives. Which is nice, in the sense that I work in a place where the patrons are comfortable claiming their sexuality openly.

And it makes me less self-conscious about ogling the handsome Black man who started using the cafe tables as his personal office this week. His name is Martin. He came in on Monday, seeming out of sorts. He ordered a drip coffee with room for cream and asked if I minded him occupying a table for a while.

I gave him the Wi-Fi password, and he settled in for the long haul. Ever since, he's sat at the corner table like a fixture for every shift I've had. I'm not sure what he's working on, but he dresses in business attire. All buttoned down shirts and freshly trimmed fade. He sometimes talks about clients, so I figure he must work in business. Just not finance like my gaming group buddies, Joel and Wes. They'd never work from a cafe for a week.

Martin drips with self-discipline. His posture is picture perfect, even when he's typing away at his laptop or clearly frustrated with the spreadsheets in his organizational binders. I've given him extra free refills as an excuse to get close and ogle the way he looks in those fitted clothes.

And I keep hearing snatches of his hushed but intense phone calls.

"It needs to be ready for the party. I've got the entire summer season booked. I can't be canceling sessions because someone who is supposed to be a professional can't get past his prejudices about my clientele." His voice, even clipped and angry, or especially when he's all stern like that, makes something in me take notice.

The snatches of one-sided conversation I overhear intensify my curiosity about what he does. What does he mean by sessions? I doubt it's true, but in my idle daydreams, the sessions are for massage, and I could be one of his clients. That has everything to do with me wanting those long elegant fingers of his working out the tension after a long week spent on my feet. And since it's a wild fantasy, the endings are a little raunchy.

Okay. A lot raunchy. I'm drawn to the idea of messing up his perfect posture and impeccable grooming. That sexy growl of his aimed at me? Fuck, yes. Thinking about my newest regular rumpled from giving me a happy ending has my dick a little too perky for the middle of my shift. So I try not to dwell on those thoughts. Much. At work.

At home? That's another story. I should probably feel bad about the number of times I've jerked off thinking about him. But I don't. He's hot, and he flirted with me first.

He's polite too, waiting until the end of a mid-afternoon rush to get his latest refill.

"Hey, hot stuff, can I get another cup?" he asks, his charming grin in place as he approaches the counter. He knows my name, greets me by it each morning, including the first one he came in, but after that, it's always hot stuff. I've only heard him use it for me, and I can't deny that the nickname makes me feel special. Silly, but there it is. I always flirt back when he uses it, calling him handsome.

"You've got it, handsome. Anything to eat with that?" I ask, because he usually gets a baked good with his afternoon coffee around this time.

"Yeah, I see you're out of my usual cookies. What would you recommend I get instead?"

"The vanilla and lavender scones are good, since you seem to like things that aren't too heavy."

"Vanilla scones, hm? Not my usual scene, but sure, I'll try one of those." His lips twitch, and his eyes shine with some secret amusement.

I lick my lips, unsure if I've somehow become the butt of a strange sense of humor. Except his expression looks more like someone sharing an inside joke. His dark eyes track the motion of my tongue. His smile turns into something more heated. It might be wishful thinking, but I get the distinct impression he wouldn't mind being the one with his tongue on my mouth. Or in it.

"Coming right up." I spin to get the pastry from the bottom of the display case set up behind me. Out of the corner of my eye, I catch him admiring my assets. Shameless flirt that I am, I linger over the scones that so happen to be on one of the lower shelves. Not that I suggested them in part for their strategic positioning. Nope, not me. I lean in to select the one from the back of the display so I can flex my glutes and let him see what he's missing.

His eyes remain locked on me when I turn to hand him his pastry on a plate. If it weren't for my work apron covering my groin, he might have gotten an eye full of how much I like him watching me. Since his eyes dipped below my belt, I dart a glance at his pants, too. It's pretty clear he liked what he saw. Good. I want him.

"It's hot today. Want to try the vanilla cold brew? It's the same price as the drip coffee." We're supposed to be pushing iced coffee to ring in summer, and the guy has got to be stifling in his suit with his constant supply of hot drinks. We might be famous for our rainy weather in the Pacific Northwest, but it's been a sunny summer so far. "What do you say? Mix things up a little?"

"Why not? I'll try it." Martin pulls out his credit card.

"Great," I ring up his order. "I'll bring it right to your table." Damn, but his ass when he walks away is a sight. The fit of his pants is doing me all the favors. More fantasy fodder for later tonight.

CHAPTER 2

Martin

Every obstacle can either be a problem or an opportunity. That's what I try to make myself believe as the obstacles keep piling up around my ears until I'm neck deep in them.

First, a pipe burst in my office above the club. Bad, but not catastrophic, until I discovered that the valve for the water shutoff rusted stuck in the 'on' position. So there was nothing I could do to minimize the water damage. Other than rescuing my computer and all the important papers before the water destroyed them, I was powerless to do anything until an emergency plumber made it to the club.

Even with the generous rate I got from Tate, a regular among my members who is a plumber, that was not cheap. And then I had to deal with emergency mitigation specialists and insurance adjusters.

Bottom line, it's been almost a month since I could open the club properly. The water left most of the private rooms unscathed. So my clientele still has places to meet up and play by appointment. Which is a large part of why they pay their membership fees. So I'm not completely ruined, but we haven't been able to have our usual parties or any sort of real public play in weeks. And with summer kicking into full swing, all my most popular events are in limbo until I can get the public rooms back in working order.

Our Midsummer Night party would have been last week, so that got canceled. The first contractor I hired took one look at the dungeon, realized what kind of club I run, and backed out of working with me. Getting a new contractor lined up on short notice during their busy season is not going well. And now Tabby is out of school, and has turned our cozy apartment into an impromptu dance studio to practice her audition pieces. So she's home all day with her music on loop, meaning I can't take over the table with all my club business. Circumstances have all but driven me from my home. And my office is still out of commission from the water damage.

I needed somewhere with internet access to work, hence I ended up here. In a cafe. They have a steady supply of coffee and what seems to be a kink and queer positive vibe. Most importantly, as long as I buy something every few hours, they let me use as much free Wi-Fi as I need and leave me to work in peace.

I've even got a bit of a casual flirtation going with the perky white barista, who makes handsome almost sound like sir. Just the right amount of demur to make me want more than our casual conversations. I've had worse work environments. This situation is an opportunity in disguise. Deep undercover levels of disguise.

It's my chance to remodel the club. Work I've put off for years. My insurance company finally agreed to pay out on my policy. Thank goodness I splurged on the top tier coverage. Tate helped me make sure I had everything documented down to the tiniest detail, so that helped expedite the claims process as much as possible.

I already had a water remediation team he recommended come in to dry everything out and prevent mold. Issues with mold might have shut down even the limited capacity Adventures still has available while I plan the remodel. Once we start construction, the private rooms will have to close too. It will be a temporary closure.

The dream I built with Charlie isn't dead. My insurance pay out means I have the capital to reinvest in the club. Now is my chance to design my dream dungeon. And unveil it at the big Summer Fling event I host every year in August.

But that won't happen if I can't get a contractor who will work with me. Barb, on my reception staff, suggested that I could put away anything that makes the club's true purpose obvious. I could, but I don't want to hide or play into their ideas that what we do is shameful. It isn't, and I refuse to be ashamed of my club or anything that happens inside its walls.

Besides, for the plans I've got in mind, I need to be sure of everyone's safety. That's not just the business owner in me wanting to avoid liability, either. It's the dominant part of me, demanding that I take care of everyone who puts their trust in me. The bottoms getting strung up from the rafters, and the tops putting them there. If we're installing permanent hardpoints for suspending people, I need to know that the structure is sound for that purpose.

So, whoever I hire has to understand what they are building. And they have to be invested in making it safe, or they aren't the contractor for me. The problem is, I'm having a hard time finding the right person for the job. And it's getting damn hard to see that as any kind of opportunity.

Bob unobtrusively slides my fresh coffee onto the table by my elbow. Bless that boy. He's so attentive to my needs. I get a vibe from him that he'd excel at giving service to a dom. He practically glows with happiness whenever I praise him.

"Thanks, hot stuff," I flash him an approving grin. He has nothing to do with my frustrations, so I shove those aside when I'm interacting with him.

"No problem, happy to be of service, handsome." His cheeky grin is hard to resist. And I can imagine what it would sound like if he called me sir instead of handsome. What would his service look like if I took him home? Or to the club?

That tight ass he made a point of showing me earlier would look glorious in leather or naked and spread open for me. Sex can't be my top priority right now. I sip the coffee, not expecting much from a flavored cold brew.

My first icy sip is unexpectedly pleasant. The sweetness is subtle and the flavors pair well with the scone he suggested. Bob got the perfect amount of cream for my tastes. The guy knows his stuff.

I sigh contentedly as I set the cup down. Bob seems to take that as a personal compliment. He's smiling to himself like the cat who got the canary as he unobtrusively wipes down the vacant table next to mine. Yeah, he isn't helping me get over my infatuation by being that happy with even that small of a sign of my pleasure with him.

It's like he's tuned into me. I'd love that attunement in a partner if I had time for a personal life. Which I don't right now. Not between Tabby graduating and the club falling apart. I've only got another hour to work before I need to get home to my daughter. She needs someone to make sure she takes a break from practicing before her blisters have blisters. But first, I've got more work.

I have one more contractor to call today. This might be lucky number ten. Or is it twelve? I could consult my notes to find out for sure, but that's demoralizing, so I don't. Instead, I gather my thoughts and make yet another call while the cafe isn't too bustling with other patrons who my hushed conversation might disturb. I don't have any better options for workspaces, so I'm stuck working with what I've got.

It's an opportunity. Make new friends, perhaps even draw some new clients. If the bits of conversation I've overheard around the cafe are what I think they are, the message board near the door might not be a terrible place to advertise the Summer Fling. Once I'm sure we won't have to cancel it.

Better make that call. The sooner I get the renovations started, the less likely my business will slowly die from the lack of a venue. And if this guy falls through, one of my friends might know someone who can help. I seem to recall Kylee having renovations done at her home over the winter, never hurts to ask.

CHAPTER 3

Bob

Martin is packing away his work things as I go to clock out at the end of my shift, the same time he's left all week. Except today I'm off the clock, whereas the past few days I was working the closing shift. So it might not be divine providence or anything, but I can spot an opportunity as well as the next horny guy.

"Hey, Martin, can I walk you out?" I ask as I round the counter to leave.

Martin glances up at me, an amused smile tugging at his lips. The same lips I've been fantasizing about all week. God, he looked amazing earlier, licking away traces of the sugary glaze from his scone. I tried to sear that image into my eyeballs to remember later. In bed. Or the shower. Martin is hot, and I could picture that glaze being something much dirtier with very little effort.

"Sure, hot stuff, you off for the day?" Martin fastens the zip on his laptop case. He picks it up by the handles, all his papers and devices already stowed inside.

"I am. So, I've got the evening free," I offer with a flirty wink.

Regret clouds his features. Guess I misread things. My face falls. There goes that vain hope. Did I truly believe a successful professional would want me for more than casual flirting?

"It's not that I don't appreciate the offer, Bob, but I have to get home."

"Boyfriend waiting for you?" I ask bitterly, because my dick seems to have a thing for men who are already attached. Looks like Martin is another in a long line of men I've wanted to fuck who had already committed to fucking someone else. Credit where it's due; he might be the first to tell me before anything goes beyond harmless flirting. I sigh, resigned to the inevitable outcome. What did I honestly expect?

"Daughter, actually." Martin corrects, a knowing smile on his gorgeous lips. Like he can read just how much his rejection stings and why I all but accused him of being unfaithful. We head for the exit. The sooner we part ways, the sooner I can work on getting him out of my head.

"Oh." I say, unsure whether to believe him.

"Tabby is nineteen. She graduated from an arts academy last week and is dead set on getting into a professional dance company. Before her tyrannical father makes her pursue a degree in something far more boring and dependable than dance as a career. Left to her own devices, she'd never take off her damn dance shoes and eat a proper meal. So I'm off to declare practice over for the day and get her fed." Martin shrugs.

He included too much detail to be pure fabrication, right? Why bother making up a kid if he's just another cheater. Far easier to take me up on my none too subtle overture, right?

Martin holds open the door to Sin and Chocolate and gestures for me to go first. That shouldn't make me all swoony and ready to forgive, but it does. I even put a bit of extra sway in my step. If he's rushing home to his kid and not a partner, it's possible there's still hope for us yet. He must be interested in me. Why else would he bother explaining himself and letting me get to know him more?

"Why send her to an arts school if you don't want her working in the arts?" I ask. It's more than carrying on the flirting, I want to know. He intrigues me, and this is our first substantive conversation. Martin walks down the block and I keep pace, even though my bus stop is in the opposite direction. I'm not giving up on my shot with him so easily if he's available. Even if he is intent on crushing dreams, both his daughter's hopes of dancing, and mine of getting him in my bed for the night.

"I have no intention of making her give up her dreams," he says, as though he can read my thoughts. "I only want Tabby to have a fall-back plan in case those dreams take an unexpected detour. Or if she gets injured. Anything can happen. I wouldn't be a very good protector if I left her unprepared for the harsher realities of the world. And anyway, we agreed that she would take a year to focus on signing with a professional company. If that doesn't pan out, she'll enroll in a degree or job training program. Which is why she has me banished from the house so she can practice instead of throwing her savings into renting studio time somewhere. Normally, I'd let her practice at Adventures in the mornings before we open to members, but well, with the renovations stalled out, that isn't an option."

"Adventures?" I repeat, swooning because this guy is too perfect to be real. The strong protector I've always dreamed about having as a partner. From the first time, my first crush shoved me into a trash can and I realized I might need someone to chase away the bad guys. And the first time I realized the hard shove, with its attendant humiliation, wasn't as much of a turnoff as it should be.

So what if Martin's old enough that his kid is probably closer to my age than he is? We're both adults. And he's got *biceps* under that button-up shirt.

"Yep. My business, we're members only. I run the place, fill in as a DM when we're short-staffed, and make sure everyone has a good time in the dungeon. My late partner opened it with me when Tabby was still in diapers. Lots of wonderful memories."

"Oh. That sounds interesting. Sorry for your loss, Martin." I run my hands lightly over his forearm, the gesture meant to be comforting.

Right after he mentions his dead spouse is not the time to ask about his business. I might look it up later. I've never played with a professional DM before, but I've heard you can hire them, if you know where to look. What are the odds a regular who offers his services as a dungeon master would fall right into my lap? This must be fate.

My game group just lost our DM, Kel, to schedule conflicts. They're all after me to run our next campaign, since they seem to think I'm swimming in free time to come up with exciting dungeons for them to explore.

It's so much pressure to run everything. I'd rather play. The same as everyone else in my group. I wonder how much Martin charges and if the group would consider paying someone to run our game.

Theo, one of our regulars at work, seems to be super into running campaigns. Maybe he'd do it? Worth considering. Or at least asking if he has any advice. Another time, like when I'm not angling to get in Martin's tailored pants.

"Thanks. Charlie's been gone a long time, but I appreciate the sentiment. So, as much as I'd love to take you up on an evening together, I've got a hungry teenager waiting for me to bring her food."

"I get it. You're a dad first, right?" I force levity into my tone, even though my chance with Martin is slipping through my fingers.

"Right. Thanks for understanding, hot stuff." Martin gently chucks my cheek and I lean into the brief contact. "This is me." He gestures to a pay-per-day parking structure a few blocks from the cafe. The kind where people get murdered in adventure movies, all shadows and concrete. Or where we might have the illusion of privacy, if I were to offer to blow him in the backseat of his car.

Classy is my middle name. Do these places have surveillance cameras? Do I care? Nope. Not enough to deter me from making the offer, anyway. If I'm honest, the idea of some anonymous security guard getting off on watching me has me all kinds of hot and bothered.

I want to taste Martin so bad and this is my chance to make an impression he won't soon forget. I'm adept at sucking cock. More to the point, I enjoy it, and it's been a while since I've met anyone I cared to pursue more than one steamy night with. I want to leave Martin wanting more, so a quick BJ might be the ticket to getting as deep under his skin as he is under mine.

"I could, uh, walk you to your car. Give you something to remember me by?" I try to make my smile and tone convey my meaning. It must work, because Martin gets that speculative look like he does when I catch him ogling my ass as if he wants to devour me.

Martin quirks his finger, beckoning me closer. I obey without conscious thought, swaying nearer to him. He takes my face in his hands and speaks low, right into my ear. "Are you offering me a quickie in my car, Bobby?" The air of command in that voice sends shivers of want up my spine.

"Yes, please." I all but whimper. I'm not a fan of the diminutive form of my name, but hearing it from Martin sends pleasant shivers up my spine. It's like he's stepping into that big domineering protector role I've fantasized about countless times. He's so fucking hot and I'm burning for him.

I lick my lips, imagining his cock parting them. This gorgeous man holding my head in place, like he is now, as he feeds me his dick an inch at a time. Fuck. My knees are wobbly already. Too bad I can't kneel right here on the sidewalk. I mean, I could, but that might cause a scene. My lips part, my eyes are half-lidded as I let the fantasy of Martin making me his plaything in broad daylight spool out in my mind.

Hot breath ghosts over my cheek, then his soft lips cover mine. Martin tastes of vanilla and coffee. His kiss is demanding, claiming my mouth and holding me in place as I all but melt into his touch.

The kiss ends far too soon, with Martin gently scraping my lower lip between his teeth, leaving me breathy and tingling from his touch. I chase his taste with my tongue. Martin puts his arm around me and guides me inside and to his car. The older model sedan has tinted rear windows, and that makes my pulse race with anticipation. We're really doing this.

Martin unlocks it and helps me into the back seat. He adjusts the driver's seat as far forward as it will slide. Oh fuck, he's making room for me to kneel in front of him. So I can suck him off. I'm so turned on that I can barely sit still waiting for him. As soon as there's enough space, I slip into the footwell and turn to face the back, palming myself through my pants. Yeah, I'm going to get lucky with my fantasy man. Fuck, yes.

"Slide over, hot stuff. You want me to take control and dominate you?" Martin nudges me over enough so he can get in with me. The command makes my blood sing, like it somehow amps everything up even more. At this rate, I'm going to shoot before I even get him in my mouth. He's just so… I don't even have words for what he does to me.

"Yes. Whatever you want, Martin. I want to blow you so bad I could scream." I shuffle to the side, making room for him to join me.

"Now, I'm sure you don't mean that, Bobby, my boy. For starters, the car lacks soundproofing, so screaming might draw undue attention. And for another, we haven't discussed your limits." Martin folds himself into the backseat and shuts the door. He adjusts us both so that I'm kneeling between his thick thighs.

"I don't want to discuss anything except how fast you can get your dick down my throat. I'm so thirsty for you. Please?" I beg, pawing at his thighs and enjoying being boxed in by his body.

"Slow down, boy." He caresses my face as he lifts his hips to shove his pants out of the way enough to free his dick. When I reach for him, greedy for my first taste, he stops me with his palm on my forehead.

"Not yet, hot stuff. Gotta suit up first." Martin softens the reminder that we aren't anything to each other by pulling my face up for another scorching kiss. I let him devour my mouth as he digs into his pocket for the rubber.

When Martin pulls back, I blink up at him, ready for him to continue taking charge of the encounter. What is it about him that makes me want to obey his commands? It could be the fact that, so far, he's only given me commands I'm desperate for already.

Martin pulls his hard dick out of his boxers. He gives himself a languid stroke along the thick length. I whimper and lean in, wanting to taste him as a bead of moisture pearls at the tip. He strokes it over his shaft before I can mouth at him, leaving a glistening trail along the path I want to follow with my tongue. His other hand, still resting on my forehead, stops me again.

My whine of desire melds into his throaty moan. I glance up at his face and I love that I'm part of putting that raw desire laced with pleasure into his hooded eyes. I want to make him get lost in bliss, like his intoxicating kisses are dragging me under his spell. His eyes open and our gazes lock.

"You ever put a condom on your partner without using your hands, boy?" Martin asks, all casual. Like he's asking about the weather, instead of one of the hottest acts I've ever considered adding to my bedroom repertoire.

"Not yet." I gaze up at him, unsure how that would work. It sounds hot as fuck, as long as I don't end up choking myself on the latex. Especially if he's volunteering his cock for me to practice this new life skill that I didn't realize I needed.

"That's a shame. Guess your homework can be to practice for next time." He rolls on the latex, then aims his sheathed cock at my mouth. "Open wide, tongue out." He caresses my cheek again, the gentle touch at odds with the firm command.

I like this bossy, gently forceful side of him during sex. The fact he knows exactly what he wants and is in control of the encounter frees me to act the wanton, giving in to my every urge. Safe in knowing that he'll stop me from being too reckless.

I open wide and he smacks his dick against my cheek before painting the smooth tip over my lips. I strain my tongue after him, trying to get a lick of my prize.

Martin chuckles. His free hand cups the back of my skull. "Such an eager boy, aren't you?"

"Give it to me, Martin, please?" I whine.

"Tell me how much you want it, hot stuff." Martin strokes himself, resting the tip against my cheek, infuriatingly close to where I want him. When I try to turn enough to take him in my mouth, his grip tightens in my hair, stopping me short. Martin grinds the tip into my face, making my lust for him that much more intense.

"Please? I've been fantasizing about going to my knees for you all week. I need to suck you, make you come. Let you fuck me. I'm so horny I'm gonna come just from having you in my mouth, please?"

"You're that thirsty for my cock?" Martin taunts, smacking it against my cheek again.

"Yes!" I whine.

"Show me." Martin lays the head of his dick on my tongue, and I let myself get lost in the singular sensation of holding another man's cock in my mouth. The hot pulse of the big vein running along the underside pressed against my tongue. The stretch of my lips to accommodate his girth.

God, that girth. I can't wait to have him in my ass someday soon. Stretching me with every thrust. I moan around him at the thought. The little reflexive thrust I get out of him in response is divine. Oh, how I love making a man come unglued with nothing but my mouth.

I run my tongue over every inch of him, adoring his cock like it's my long-lost love. He controls how deep I take him. It drives me wild to be held in place with him nudging at the back of my throat. I work him, alternating suction and licking as much as I can with Martin taking control of the blow job.

I've never experienced anything this mind-numbingly hot before in my life. It's like he's taking everything I want to give him and I can't help the soaring exaltation that I have exactly what this man wants. That I can give him all the pleasure in the world just by kneeling before him and offering myself up to him.

"That's it. Can you take it all the way?"

"Mhm," I moan in an affirmative and press against him, eager to show him I can do what he wants.

I gag a little the first time he pushes into my throat. It's not that he takes me by surprise or that I haven't had practice deep throating, it's a novel experience when I'm not in control of the motions involved. When he's holding me in place and taking everything I offer him. He backs off and lets me suck on him for a while before making me take him all the way to the root again. This time, I know what's coming and I open up for his entire length, swallowing around him.

"That's it, boy, open up for me." Martin strokes my face with his hands. How is that touch more intimate than his dick shoving past my tonsils? "Let me in." His hands on me are reverent as his dick fills my throat. "Let me have all of you."

He fucks my face in slow, sensual strokes, and somehow, it feels like I'm something special. Something to treasure and claim. Like he's flipping the entire script on me. Instead of my worshipping his dick, it's him worshipping my mouth and throat with every shift of his hips. He's giving me an offering that I crave with every fiber of my being. And I'm floaty and lust-drunk at the weight of it all.

By this point, I'd give my left nut for a bit of friction. It's so achingly good I can hardly stand another second before I fly off into bliss. The reality of sex with Martin is even hotter than my fantasies. Until tonight, I've never admitted, even to myself, how I crave this. To be so utterly controlled by a lover during sex. But I'm so turned on, I think I could almost come untouched from having him take me like this.

When I reach for myself, unable to resist any longer, Martin clamps his hand around my wrist. "Not like that," he grunts, keeping my palm pressed firmly to his meaty thigh. I feel every bunch and stretch of his muscles as he thrusts into me. "You aren't getting yourself off." He moans as he pushes deeper into my throat, filling all of my senses. The next time he slides back out to let me draw in a breath, he shifts so that his ankle is resting between my legs. His bony shin presses against my rock hard erection. "You're getting off on me, boy. Because it's what I want. Don't you forget it." Martin nudges his ankle more firmly against me.

I'm far too horny to balk at getting off by humping his leg. So that's how I come. Riding his shin like Martin has me so lost to lust that he's pushed me past any shame, there's no room for that through the haze of desire.

The spreading warmth as my cum soaks into my pants barely distracts me from his balls mashing against my chin. Martin moans and grunts through his own release, driving in as deep as

I can take him. I strain to keep Martin cradled inside me as long as he'll allow. Knowing I made him come drives another gush spurting out of my balls, my dick twitches almost painfully at the prolonged orgasm. The sounds I make around his cock might form some garbled version of his name. It's all over far too soon.

Martin eases his cock free. I rest my face against his thigh. He strokes my hair.

"I knew you'd be hot stuff in bed, Bobby."

"Mhm," I mumble, savoring the stolen moment of closeness as he lets me rest in his lap. Far too soon, he nudges my face away.

"Was I good?" I ask, fishing for more praise now that the immediate feedback of his obvious pleasure in the act is over. Martin ties off the condom and tucks himself back into his pants.

He pauses, cupping my face in his hands and kissing me one more time. I could get stuck on the sensation of his lips moving against mine. Best kisser I've been with in ages. One of the few who keeps up the charade of affection after the cum cools. When it ends, I gaze up at him, all moony eyed with post-orgasmic bliss.

"You were wonderful, Bobby." He sounds so sincere that there isn't any room to doubt he means it. He liked it too. "Come here." Martin pulls me up onto the seat beside him. He opens his arms and lets me snuggle into his embrace. He holds me while the worst of the panicky adrenaline crash hits. I wish I could have him hug me for hours, but I offered him a quickie and getting clingy afterward is a sure way to scare him off from a repeat. I pull away long before I'm ready to let go.

"Next time, I'll plan on having more time to assure you that you are wonderful for as long as you need. But tonight, I have to get home. Will you be alright if I drop you off somewhere? The cafe or someplace a friend can meet you?"

"Can you drop me off at home? It's not far." Could I sound more needy? This is why my exes say I'm clingy. I just get like this after exceptional sex sometimes.

If it's only a BJ or a quick hard fuck, I'm fine. But the best sex pushes me to try new situations, and that's when I get weepy and shaky like this. Needing reassurances and pampering after I let them do whatever they want to me. Everything from oral that left me gasping for breath, to an erotic spanking, to the ex who asked to pee on me. I wanted those things too.

I always want it. It's not like I go along with sexual situations I don't enjoy. But I need my partner, however temporary, to want me afterward. Most times, they don't. I hope Martin isn't like that. I shiver a little. The wet patch in my pants is getting cold and stickily uncomfortable. Not the first time I've shuffled home with cum soaked pants. Unlikely it will be the last either.

"I can drop you at home if you're sure you want to give me your address already." Already. He's talking like he wants to see me again. That holds the melancholy part of me at bay for the moment.

"It's fine. I want to see you again. This will make it easy for you to find me." I shrug like it's no big deal. It isn't. I've invited home plenty of hookups I didn't know as well as him. He's probably accustomed to exercising caution because he has a kid to worry about.

"Okay. Why don't you clean up, climb into the front and punch the address into the GPS for me." Martin presses a wad of clean tissues into my hand.

I nod. Having what to do next all spelled out for me isn't necessary, but it's nice. And having a task to do distracts me from the disproportionate let down of Martin fucking and running on me.

CHAPTER 4

Martin

I spend far too much time thinking about Bob after I drop him off outside his place. He rebuffed my offer to walk him to his door, even though he still seemed shaky after we fucked. He was so into letting me take control that I didn't give enough consideration to how far I might have pushed him past his usual limits.

To be fair, I've overheard him having conversations that imply he's not inexperienced. He'd asked for everything we did, but it still doesn't sit well that I left him on his own when he was showing signs of having an endorphin crash. If it weren't for Tabby waiting at home, I might have pressed the issue more. But Bob said he didn't want me to stay, so he must have a system for dealing with a crash.

Besides, Tabby had texted, wondering why I was late, and I hate making her worry. So I gave Bob my number and made him promise to call if he needed to talk or anything. He snorted about how overprotective I was being and left. He took my number, though.

It's a relief to walk into Sin this morning and see his smiling face behind the counter as usual. Is it my imagination, or does his cheesy customer service smile brighten when our eyes meet? The surreptitious up-down he gives me with his eyes isn't my imagination at all. I smirk at him and give him a much slower perusal. His work apron smooths out his wiry physique, that's a pity.

Our eyes meet and he winks, mouthing 'later' to me. "Good morning, how can I help you sin today?" He delivers a cheesy line that's a play on the shop name. I've noticed the baristas using it to joke around with their regulars. Guess I'm fast becoming one of those.

"Coffee. Better make it a double shot. I didn't sleep well last night." I sidle up to the counter.

"Oh? Something wrong with all the plans you've been fussing over?" Bob gestures toward my usual table, his eyes soft and sympathetic.

"No, nothing like that." It's on the tip of my tongue to tell him I stayed up worrying about him and reliving our backseat blowjob. But I don't want to spook him by getting too intense, too fast. Just because I enjoy taking care of my scene partners almost as much as the scene itself doesn't mean he wants that from me. Besides, what we did barely counts as a scene.

I mean, technically there was some mild breath play involved with choking him on my dick. But it's not like I was actually cutting off his airways anymore than the norm for oral sex. Other than his sweet and willing ceding of control to me, it was downright vanilla. Like his coffee, and the flavor of our shared kiss.

"What is it like then?" Bob asks, inviting me to trust him.

"I've got a lot on my mind." I shrug, pretending not to notice the way his smile dampens when I decide not to take him into my confidence. Bob is too perceptive not to realize my answer is a brush off, but the last thing my hectic summer needs is more complications.

We exchange the obligatory niceties as he takes my order, and I still can't tear my eyes off him, even if my heart isn't in flirting this morning. He offers to bring my coffee and breakfast pastry right over when it's ready. Since I timed my arrival for after the worst of the Friday morning rush, I don't feel guilty about taking him up on it. I stuff a tip in the jar and set up my work area for the day.

I need to get Bobby out of my head and pull my business back from the brink of ruin. Not to mention making sure Tabby takes care of herself while she shoots for the stars. I'm not ready for my baby to be all grown up and leaping out of the nest, heedless of how far she might fall.

I'm not dwelling on that. One crisis at a time. Tabby has auditions with several dance companies coming up and I'll fly her all over creation to make sure she can follow her dreams. Even if it kills me to keep the club solvent enough to make that promise a reality.

I'm overreacting. Adventures does well. Membership hasn't suffered from the water damage shutting down our main public play area, yet. I can turn this into a positive. I just need to find the right contractor to transform my dreams into reality.

That's the way my thoughts are running when I get a call back from the contractor one of my regulars recommended. After all my fruitless searching, I finally got wise and reached out to my community for help. It should have been my first move, but the entire situation with the business has me frazzled.

Kylee used this guy for a home remodel she did a while back. She and her pup wanted some custom work done. The guy they hired wasn't in the lifestyle, but he was kink positive. Not to mention discreet about the custom work he did for them. Quent, Kylee's pup, even struck up a friendship with the guy, according to her. I left him a message last night after I got home, so the fact he is calling me back so promptly has to be a good sign about his professionalism.

"Hello?" I answer the call, excited at the name on the caller ID, but not wanting to overwhelm him.

"Hello. This is Harry Reynolds, with Reynolds Construction. I'm calling for Martin Keyes?"

"Yeah, Martin speaking."

"Great. So, your message mentioned that one of my residential clients recommended me for your commercial renovation?"

"Yes. I know this might not be up your alley, but Kylee mentioned how accepting you were of her and her partner's lifestyle. So I thought it was at least worth reaching out and seeing if you could help me, or point me toward a colleague with similar views?"

"You're in luck, Mr. Keyes. I specialize in commercial work. I remember the remodel in question. That was a favor for a friend. I had a break in my schedule and the timing worked. I'm always happy to help kinksters in need. My folks were active in the community. So, what can I do for you? You mentioned water damage?"

"Right. Had a pipe burst, and the assessor says that the main event space is a total gut job. I'm still able to use the front half of the building, but the back wall where the pipe burst is an issue. I'll need you to ensure the entire space's structural integrity and redo the offices upstairs. My plumber already took care of refitting all the worn out pipes and the mitigation team assures me there isn't any mold or rot. We need to redo the main event room and create a lounge area. I've got plans all drawn up, and permits handled. We've been meaning to update the space for a while, so I'm hoping we can take advantage of the repairs to turn it into the dungeon of my dreams. We're talking, every one of my clients leaves every session dreaming of coming back for more."

"I can make that happen for you. Do you have the design drawn up with exactly what you want? Or do you need help with drafting the plans?"

"I've got the blueprints. If we can meet to discuss them ASAP, that would be fantastic. I've got a big annual summer party planned for mid-August, and in an ideal world, that's when I want to do our grand reopening."

"So, we've got around eight weeks? Might be a tight timeline, depending on the project's scope and your budget. Why don't we plan to meet at the site so I can see what we're dealing with. Bring along your plans and I'll see what I can do for you, and get a quote for you early next week. Sound good?"

"Sounds perfect."

I give him the address, and we hang up with plans to do a site walkthrough this afternoon. And with one fortuitous call, my luck has turned a corner. We might not have to cancel the entire summer event schedule after all.

CHAPTER 5

Bob

Martin doesn't act much differently the morning after we screwed around in his car. It's Friday, though, and part of me wonders if this is the last day he'll be coming into the cafe. He spent all week here to stay out of Tabby's hair, but how long does he intend to work from Sin?

I don't want to be overfamiliar by asking, but I'm even more distracted by him than usual. I catch myself drinking in my fill of his long elegant fingers cupped around his mug every time he sips his coffee. And the way his throat bobs when he swallows. The furrow in his brow as he puzzles over whatever is on his screen. His gorgeous smile when he hangs up from that conversation about designing his dream dungeon.

I don't try to listen in on his work conversations, but he makes the call after the morning rush of commuter traffic fizzles away. It's quiet without a crowd in the cafe. So I can't help overhearing him while I'm cleaning off the nearby tables. He mentions the importance of the people he works with being queer friendly. And he's talking about designing custom dungeons for his party. How cool would it be to play in a game with someone like Martin, who pays attention to the little details that make the game shine?

I am already deeply in lust with this guy. The fact he shares my taste in leisure activities is enough to have my hopes for more than a quickie in his backseat soaring somewhere near the stratosphere. It's silly to get emotionally invested after one orgasm. Even if blowing him did sort of blow my mind.

The lunchtime rush takes my mind off Martin for a while. In the middle of the ravening horde clamoring for their afternoon pastries and coffee, Martin packs up to leave. That's a break from his regular pattern. He catches my eye and waves. I'm too busy to do more than shoot him a return wave, even as my heart sinks at the thought he might not be back.

By the time the crowd thins to a trickle of customers, Martin is long gone. Several teenagers enjoying their summer break are lingering at his table. I mope around for most of my remaining shift, grumpy that I missed my shot for a repeat of last night.

Two of the guys from my gaming group swing by the cafe after the lunch rush, breaking up the monotony of missing Martin. Technically they're my friends, though recently that seems more nominal than real. Joel is an average white guy with an inflated ego. Wes has the lean musculature of a cyclist and a golden complexion. He's the more laid back of the pair.

Their presence here only serves to remind me I want more than just another BJ with Martin. I want his expertise at the game table, too. Joel and Wes work together not too far from here, so it's not unheard of for them to come by for their afternoon coffee.

"Oh, hey, I wasn't expecting you two today. Couldn't wait until tonight to see me?" I bat my eyes at them, flirting for the fun of it, since they're usually good sports about playing along. We have game tonight, our second session in a while. Haley put together a one-off for us to play last week since all of us are jonesing for a new game. The one shot turned into two. It's her first time DMing, so we all cut Haley some slack, but it's been a bit of a bumpy ride.

Joel and Wes exchange a weighted glance. Uh oh, I'm sensing an ulterior motive for this social call.

"Long lunch, we were in the area and needed a quick minute with you in private," Joel rolls his shoulders and tips his chin at the specials board. "Vanilla cold brew?"

"Yep, that's our monthly special." I nod. "Cold brew to celebrate the warmer weather while it lasts. Is that what you want?"

"Sure, get me a medium, please." Wes smiles. He's the nicer of the pair.

The chime above the door announces a new arrival. When I glance over to greet the customer with a canned welcome, my heart flutters as I realize it's Martin, returning from whatever errand called him away earlier. He waves as he queues up behind Joel and Wes.

Joel clears his throat to recall my attention to him.

"Sorry, what can I get you, Joel? Same as Wes?" I let his irritation roll off my back with an effort.

"Nah, too vanilla for me," he winks like it's a joke. "How about a hazelnut cappuccino?"

"Sure, coming right up." They pay, and I turn to make their drinks.

"Here you go, enjoy," I force a smile, hoping they aren't here to pressure me about our game again.

Wes thanks me and steps to the side. Joel leans across the counter, ignoring Martin waiting behind him.

"Look," Joel taps his forefinger against the countertop, like he needs to get my attention or something, even though I'm a captive audience since he ambushed me at work. "Have you considered what we suggested?" Joel asks.

"I don't know, man. I'm not sure I'm up to running things. It's an enormous commitment." I comb my fingers through my hair, then wince because I'm not supposed to do that while I'm working with the orders. Joel is stressing me out with the high-pressure tactics he's been using for weeks now to get me to agree. I'll need to wash my hands before the next customer. "I don't enjoy the responsibility. Besides, Haley agreed to try DMing. Why not give her a chance?"

"You're better at it. She's too quick to jump in and control things. It takes everyone out of the scene, you know?"

I sigh, he's not wrong. Haley has already displayed an irritating habit of railroading the party to the conclusions she has planned instead of adapting to how her scenarios play out with the party. She's just new and needs practice. I had similar struggles with the first few campaigns I ran.

Joel's mostly mad because his character bore the brunt of some bad rolls last week. Rolls a more experienced DM would have fudged to keep the game moving. Or at least, our old one, Kel, would have. Joel isn't fun to play with when he's sulking.

"You're the best person for the job, Bob. No one else has the amount of free time you do to organize things. Haley means well, but she's not the best fit for the group." Joel cajoles.

I sigh, frustrated that he is so hung up on me taking over now that Kel is out of the picture. Wes isn't half as bad, but he isn't contradicting Joel, either. "Can we talk later? I'm at work." I gesture toward the cafe, like it's not obvious. Joel rolls his eyes and huffs out a breath.

"It's not like you're busy right now."

"I have a customer waiting behind you. Let me get his order and then I can take a break to talk, okay?" I say through clenched teeth. I met Joel and the others during my one semester at university. It only took one term for me to decide university, and its attendant debt, wasn't for me. I withdrew in time to get most of my loans refunded and I got a regular gaming group out of that semester.

If it weren't such a hassle to find new groups now that I'm done with school, I'd have ditched these guys ages ago. but I want a steady gaming group more than I want to be done with Joel's BS. So I stick around despite all the snide little remarks he makes about my job and what a slacker I am compared to Joel and Wes's work in finance. They weren't such dicks back in school. Wes still isn't. He has the grace to look embarrassed about Joel's behavior, shifting nervously from foot to foot and sipping on his drink to avoid getting drawn into our terse discussion.

"Fine." Joel gives a sharp nod. "We'll grab a table, I guess. What's five more minutes." He storms off. Wes gives me a sympathetic look, and a mouthed apology before he follows. I turn to wash up and give myself a minute to breathe, so I'm not a flustered mess in front of Martin.

Martin steps up to the counter. "Sorry to interrupt, that seemed intense."

I wave it off as I dry my hands. "Not at all. I'm sorry you had to wait. Didn't expect you back today, everything alright?"

"Couldn't stay away from you for long, Bobby." Martin's gaze roves over my body with obvious appreciation. It makes me hot all over that he seems to like what he sees. He wants more of me. Good. Wonderful, even. "Just had to meet a contractor at Adventures to discuss the remodel. It's going to make for an epic play area once it's complete. And I found the perfect guy for the work, it's been a hassle finding someone willing to embrace working with our community."

I grimace sympathetically, well aware of how deep prejudice can go, though maybe not on the same levels as Martin. It's cool that he is so committed to making his business inclusive like that, though. "I'm glad you found a good fit for the job. What can I get you to celebrate?"

"You've got me hooked on your seasonal ice coffee, that and the scones." Martin reaches for his wallet and I hold up a hand to forestall him.

"On me, as a congrats."

"Are you sure?" he hesitates, hand poised over his pocket. He must see in my expression how much it means to me to do something for him, because he doesn't push the issue.

"I'm positive. You've been so stressed, let me do something nice for you." I give him a hopeful look.

"Thanks, Bobby, I appreciate it." Martin flashes me a soft smile. He looks like he wants to lean across the counter and kiss me, but he doesn't give in to that temptation. I flash him a smile and turn to serve him, unleashing every bit of swish in my step and letting him ogle my assets.

I glance at Martin over my shoulder and it's hella validating to see he can't seem to tear his eyes away from me while I'm working. I give him a cheesy wink, and he chuckles and shakes his head at me. When I hand him his order, he thanks me and walks away. The teens are still at his usual table, so he takes the one next to where Joel and Wes are loitering. Joel is watching me with a raised brow, his expression showing he is unimpressed at the holdup. I take off my apron with a resigned sigh and go to deal with him.

"Okay, I'm alone until my coworker gets back from his lunch break, so if there's a customer we'll have to cut this short." I lay out the ground rules as I approach the table. Clear boundaries are key when dealing with entitled pricks like Joel.

"That's fine. This conversation shouldn't take long," Joel replies. "Look, I know Haley means well, but you're a more experienced DM. No one wants to hurt her feelings, but come on! You know you'd be better at it than her. Do it for the party?" Joel says.

"I get that, but I think you're being too harsh. Haley has been coming around for years. She knows what she's doing, and she cares about making it good for everyone. It's only a matter of learning where to adhere strictly to the rules and where it's okay to let things slide a little as long as everyone is having fun. And

I don't enjoy DMing. I would much rather play when we all get together. It's not for me. Being the one calling the shots doesn't come naturally to me," I explain.

I glance toward Wes, hoping I might sway him to my side on this. Joel has already decided not to take no for an answer and nothing short of getting his way will satisfy him.

"It's your call. We can't force you to do it if you aren't interested." Wes shrugs. "For what it's worth, I had fun last year when you set up that gauntlet challenge for us to play at your place, when Kel was sick."

"Exactly!" Joel throws an arm around my shoulders and gives me a gentle shake that I think he means to convey solidarity. It feels more like an invasion of my personal space and an attempt at manipulation than a friendly gesture, though. I shrink away from him as he continues to blow smoke up my ass. "That predicament you set up for us was awesome. You really made us all work for the happy ending, you know? You've got a devious mind, when you apply yourself. At least consider giving it another shot?"

It would be easier in the short run to give in, but that will mean hours of pouring my heart and soul into making a campaign for this guy. Joel raves that he loved my last session now, but while we were playing, all he did was complain. He maintains that I included too many puzzles and not enough combat. So I know he won't appreciate the sort of campaign I would enjoy running. We aren't the best fit anyway, but having an imperfect gaming group is better than nothing. Or at least, it was.

Now that I know Martin is in the business of DMing, perhaps I've found a perfect alternative. Even if I have to pay to play with him. It might sting my pride to pay for stuff I'd normally do with a group of friends, but no less than having to endure Joel's constant barbs about service workers. And really, there's nothing wrong with paying for a service I need, right?

The teens in the corner are getting up and eyeing the menu

board, so I've got to wrap up our little chat.

"Look, I'll think about it, and we can see how Haley does tonight. Give her a real chance. But I have to work now." I push back my chair and notice that Martin is still sitting right there. I wonder how much he overheard? Doesn't matter, we've both overheard enough of each other's conversations that I'm pretty sure he already realizes we've got plenty of shared interests beyond giving each other orgasms.

"No problem. We ought to hit the office, too." Wes offers me a fist bump and I give it to him, even though my heart isn't in it. I sense Martin's eyes on me. Does he want me as much as I want him? "See you tonight, man." Wes salutes me with his half full coffee cup.

"Yep, later, guys," I say with all the false cheer I can muster on a Friday afternoon at the tail end of a demanding work week.

"See you tonight," Joel grumbles, his grip on his cup tight. He seems less than willing to take a hint, but he lets Wes shepherd him out of the cafe. Getting him out of my hair is all that matters. I have plenty of practice ignoring crappy attitudes in my line of work.

The teens sidle up to the counter, chattering amongst themselves. I get my apron back in place and wash up before getting their refills to go. After that, it's only another couple hours behind the coffee bar until my shift ends. I may or may not spend most of that time ogling Martin. It's quite the ego boost to realize that, more often than not, he's eyeing me right back.

CHAPTER 6

Martin

There isn't any genuine need to return to the cafe after my meeting with Harry. Sure, there are some administrative tasks that have fallen by the wayside while I've been dealing with the immediate crisis, but nothing that wouldn't keep until next week. My meeting with the contractor went well. Better than I'd hoped, even. He agreed to work with my existing plans too, which takes a load of stress off.

I could have stuck around the club to get a start on the demolition work that Reynolds gave me the go ahead to begin. It's an easy way to save on labor costs. But I'd rather keep the mess as contained as possible, so that will mean getting plastic sheeting taped up to keep the mess in. Mostly, I'll tear out damaged drywall with a few of my staff. Reynolds said that was fine for us to tackle without him as none of the walls we discussed tearing out are load-bearing, thank goodness. Another sign that the burst pipe was an opportunity in disguise.

There isn't anything at Adventures that can't wait until next week, though. I need to pick up tools this weekend, including a wire finder to be on the safe side with tearing into things. Besides, I've got several private bookings for the undamaged play rooms over the weekend to consider. No sense kicking up construction dust before I have to. Our eight week timeline will be tight, but the rest of today will be better spent organizing the details so we can hit the ground running on Monday.

Next week is soon enough to get my hands dirty. I can spend the afternoon arranging the most efficient way to achieve that. Call in my staff to see who wants to help for a bit of overtime pay. I can order a dumpster to haul everything away just as easily from Sin and Chocolate. So, I head back to the cafe after my meeting with Reynolds. I'm letting my desire to see Bobby again drive me.

My intention was to wrap up all the planning to tear things down ASAP. The sooner we do the bits we can, the sooner I can have Reynolds remake the space into my dream dungeon. The vision Charlie and I shared, but never quite had the funds to bring entirely to fruition. When the club's finances leveled out after I paid off our mortgage on the building, I didn't have the heart to change the legacy she left behind. Everything falling into place seems like a sign from her to give up my sentimentality. The renovation would thrill Charlie.

Before the end, she told me that if I didn't let myself move on without her, she'd kick my ass in whatever afterlife we might share. I'd laughed it off, joking about us having different destinations if mainstream religion has the right of things.

Charlie never had time for judgmental bullshit, religious or otherwise. She'd gotten me on my knees, calling her Ma'am and showing her how angelic I could be. That night stands out in my memories as a goodbye. One of the last she was strong enough for sex, with her telling me there was no place in hell for me, no matter how sinful my lips on her felt. Even through the pain of her illness. The memory of her putting me in my place brings a bittersweet smile to my lips.

It's been a long time since I could smile at memories of Charlie. But today, as I let fantasies of Bobby distract me from my task for the umpteenth time this week, the ache of loss has a bittersweet edge. I can't quite laugh about it, but the pain is no longer too raw to even smile about. I can remember her without it tearing my heart out all over again. And I can consider what she'd say about me rushing back over here because I'm sweet on the cute barista who is watching me with fuck-me eyes. She'd tell me that life is too damn short to fuss over what makes me happy.

If dominating a younger man gets me back into the dating game, she'd be all for it. Charlie used to love playing out scenes like that. We sometimes played with other people, or invited a third into our bed. She always got a kick out of how differently I approach taking a dominant role. I always knew my place with her. On my knees beside her, adored and adoring, even when she watched me scening with someone else. I've known I was a switch since before I learned there was a word for it. I enjoy dominance and submission. Charlie was a domme through and through. She understood I needed both, and we made it work.

I still miss her, might always miss her, but the ache isn't the echoing void it once was. There's room to let someone else into my heart now. Not as a sub again, though. I don't have it in me to give my full submission to someone else. For a scene to scratch an itch, sure, but not the dynamic that Charlie and I shared. I promised that part of me would always be for her. 'Til death, and it turns out, even after.

But the dominant side of my nature that she loved to nurture is still there. Recently, it's easier to scene with old friends and newbies at the club who need an experienced partner to guide them. The role of dom is a part of me I've grown into. One I want to explore more with Bobby, if he'll have me.

From our brief encounter last night, our tastes seem compatible. The discussion he had with his friends about a play party he's involved with planning only bolsters my suspicions. Even considering the sexy predicaments I could put him in once we finish the remodel is enough to have my mind thoroughly in the gutter. Nowhere near the work-related planning that I intended to get a jump start on before I call it quits for the day.

I buckle down and get the most urgent tasks completed while he works.

It doesn't take long once I buckle down and focus. Tabby still won't be ready to hang up her dance shoes and give up the living area of our home for another few hours. I have time to take a walk. It might clear my head. As I'm standing and stretching and debating whether to keep going or finish up my tasks tomorrow, Bobby steps out from behind the counter. His apron is no longer in evidence.

"You done for the day?" I ask, surprised at my good fortune.

"Yep. Perks of taking a morning shift. I get to head home mid-afternoon. If I didn't have a shift tomorrow it'd be even better, kicking off the weekend early." Bobby gives me a cheeky grin. "What about you? Are you abandoning your post already?" He gestures at the table that's been my de facto office all week.

"I'm taking a breather. I figured a walk might help me focus."

"Ah. Well, I don't have anywhere to be for hours. Do you want company?" Bob angles himself toward me, his coy smile and steady eye contact coupled with his tone make the subtext crystal clear.

I lick my lips and nod. "I'd love the pleasure of your company. Give me a second to pack up?" I'm already scooping up my files and stuffing everything back into my computer case to deal with later.

"Sure, no rush." Bob sidles over to my table. He clears my cup away as I zip my bag and check to be sure I'm not forgetting anything.

"You don't have to get that," I protest.

"No big deal," he replies, setting the dirty cup in the bin where they collect them. "You ready?"

"Yep," I turn toward the exit. As I expect, Bob falls into step beside me, both of us calling out farewells to his coworker behind the counter.

We've only made it a few paces toward the parking garage before Bob slips his hand into mine. "If you don't need to work, we could find more interesting ways to burn off excess energy?" Bobby glances over at me, biting his lip, then away again, like he's uncertain we're on the same page.

"Are you inviting me back to your place to fuck, hot stuff?" I give his hand a playful tug.

"Yeah, I guess that's exactly what I'm saying. If you'd be into that?"

"I'd love to take you home and make you come until you can't see straight, Bobby. There's nothing I'd enjoy more."

Bob gazes at me with open lust and I tip his chin up for a quick kiss. I twine our fingers and lead him to my car. Once we're buckled in, I decide we may as well start the fun early.

"Care to play a game on the way home?" I suggest. I'll hold off on broaching the topic of a proper scene until later. For now, we're only hooking up for casual sex, but a little something to spice things up can't hurt. What I have in mind is pretty tame, anyway.

"You mean a sex game, right?" Bob grins.

"Yes." I stroke his thigh.

Bob shifts in his seat. "Sounds fun, tell me what to do."

"I was hoping you'd say that. Here." I set my bag on his lap and he gives me a questioning look. "Hold onto that for me. Oh, and I want you to get your dick out and stroke it. Get yourself ready to come by the time we arrive, but don't come until I give you permission, got it? It would be a real shame if you got your cum all over my bag."

"Oh, yeah? What if I did? Would you punish me?" He bats his eyes at me.

"Why? Do you want me to turn you over my knee and spank your tight little ass before I fuck you?" I give him a 'try me' look. The one that makes the subs I play with listen, and Tabby roll her eyes at me.

For a moment I think I might have misread Bobby, but then he swallows hard, and the little whine he lets out goes right to my balls. "Oh, fuck. You're going to kill me with all this hotness," he moans as he lifts his hips to get his pants out of the way, one hand on my bag to steady it.

I love that he's in a rush to obey me. I make a show of adjusting my mirrors as a pretext to sit there watching him get his dick out. He's pretty, already semi-hard and flushed at the tip. I casually lick my palm and reach over to give him a few brisk pumps to get it all the way up. Bobby yelps and humps into the touch, moaning and grabbing my forearm like he never wants me to stop. The need to keep my bag steady on his knees seems to frustrate him, adding another layer to the game. I give him one more stroke, with a bit of a twist that's got to border the line between too much and not enough.

Bob whimpers, slumping in his seat and panting for breath. "Fuck, you're good at that."

"You like it rough, Bobby boy?" I grab the travel sized lube I stashed in the car after last night's interlude out of the glove box and wiggle it in front of him.

"Yeah, but I never turn down extra lube either." He reaches for the bottle.

"Get to it." I release the bottle into his hand and Bob drizzles a bit of slick onto his palm.

I watch his face as his hand closes over the sensitized skin. His eyelids slide shut and his lips part as he arches back in his seat. My bag tips forward, saved from tumbling into the footwell by the dashboard.

"Is it good?" I ask, to split his focus further and keep him from coming far too soon and ending my fun.

"Yeah. I like your hand better, though," he hints, voice low, like he isn't sure he's allowed to ask for what he wants. We can work on that.

"There's plenty more of that waiting for you at home. Keep stroking. Don't you stop until you have permission, understand?"

"Yeah. You want me pleading either way, huh?" he grunts and slows his pace. Bobby makes such a pretty picture with the flushed head of his cock poking up out of his fist.

"That's the idea." I agree. "Keep jerking it, nice and steady, no slacking off on the job." I adjust my computer bag, propping it on his thighs to give him room to stroke himself, while still having the bag obscure the view through the windshield from any passersby as we drive. The tinted windows in the back would protect his privacy more, but I want to make this harder for him. And I want to at least be able to glance over at his face while he tries to obey me, even if the bag angled over his lap obscures the view for me as well. "Go ahead."

Bob does, one hand steadying the bag and the other moving awkwardly along his length under it. I have to tear my eyes off of him to focus on driving.

This might be as much torture for me as it is for him, listening to the low grunts and stifled moans of pleasure he makes beside me. I can ignore the alluring sight of Bobby's features softened by lust for a few minutes if it means getting him home safe and driving him wild at the same time.

I remember the way to his place. It's not far, so I take a route with more traffic lights and throw in a few extra laps around his block to drag out our game. It's a joy to listen to the slick slide of his hand on his dick and the occasional thumps when he bumps my bag with his fist.

Every time we have to stop, I steal a glance at the ruddy flush of his cheeks. His sex face makes me want to kiss him breathless and fuck him all night long. The breathy moans and groans at every red light and wrong turn have us both on edge, as intended. I don't have to be able to see him jerking off to enjoy that he's doing it for me. By the time I'm ready to park the car, he's a babbling mess.

"Oh please, I'm so close. Please, Martin, I need to come. I need you to touch me. If you don't let me stop, I'm going to nut all over your fancy upholstery. Please?"

"Keep going." I pull into a metered parking spot near his building. Far enough that he'll have a bit of a walk with his dick aching for release.

"Ngh. Please, Martin?" Bobby whines with need, like he might burst if I make him wait any longer. Good.

"Please what?" I demand, tone brooking no nonsense. I get out my phone and pull up the parking app to pay for the spot. Martin groans, at my delay tactics. I glance over to admire his dick again, glistening with lube and precum as he continues to stroke.

"Please let me?" Bob whines, his hand still keeping up the rhythmic stroking I demanded of him under the bag.

"Let you what?" I press.

"I don't know!" He snaps, then sobs again, "please?"

"Do you want to come or stop touching yourself?" I ask, amused at how flustered he sounds and turned on at his easy obedience to the rules I gave him.

"Whichever you want, Martin."

I moan at that. God, it's heady that he wants to give himself to me like this. That he's into my games. I return his raw honesty in kind. "I love how much you want to please me, boy. Good boys get rewards. You can either finish jerking off now or put yourself away and I'll help you come when we get inside. Either way, that won't be the only orgasm I ask you to give me today. Is that agreeable?"

"Yes. Fuck." Bob squeezes his dick, his eyes pressed shut as he fights for control.

"I want your answer, boy. Come now or inside?"

"Inside." He breathes out hard.

"Good. Let's go." I take back my computer bag and step out of the car onto the empty sidewalk. Bobby flushes at the sudden exposure, wincing as he tucks himself away. He hobbles out of the car like he's so on edge it physically pains him.

It's intoxicating that I can get him so deep into a scene with only my commands and his own hand. The boy clearly craves this, and I hardly dare to imagine how far he'll let me push him once we've discussed limits and plan more involved scenes. If he wants that. I hope like hell that he does.

"Take me to your apartment," I instruct when he just stands there for too long collecting himself and leaning on the car door. Bobby nods and pushes away from the car. I take his arm and let him lead me to his home while he leans into my side.

I'm more than ready to deliver on my promise by the time he unlocks the door to let us into his apartment. It's a sparsely furnished studio. I take in the space at a glance and direct Bob over to his bed.

"Sit down and let me see that pretty cock again," I nod toward his groin. He sits on the edge of the mattress and I make quick work of pulling off his pants. He clings to my shoulders when I wedge myself between his knees to roll the condom onto his cock. I slipped it into my pocket this morning, in case we got a repeat of last night. I pull back to admire him, all suited up and ready to roll. Drawing out the anticipation is always more fun, so I make him wait a minute. My warm breaths play over his sensitive flesh.

Before I can take him into my mouth, Bobby puts a hand on my forehead, gently holding me back. “Oh, god, if you’re planning to blow me, I sure hope our game is over. I can’t hold off for long with your mouth on me.” His dick twitches inches from my mouth. I could reach out my tongue and lick him if I was the type to ignore his clear hesitation.

“You don’t have to hold off. I said you could come when we got inside, didn’t I?” I meet his gaze and let him see me lick my lips.

His eyes lock onto my tongue and his lips part as he mirrors the movement. “Yeah. You did. Okay.” He nods and moves his hand to my shoulder.

“You want me to suck your dick, hot stuff?” I ask, waiting until I have clear consent to move forward.

“Yes, pl-eeeease.” His voice notches up in pitch as I do exactly that, the word drawing out as he curls around me, then arches back. His hands move from my shoulders to clutch at the back of my head. He holds me against him as he gives a little involuntary thrust of his hips to meet me. “Oh, fuck.” His tortured moans as he tries to hold out are music to my ears.

I interpret his cursing as encouragement and take him deeper. He loosens his hold enough to let me move along his shaft. I stroke the base with my fist as I lavish attention on the head and take him deep again by turns. True to his word, he doesn’t last long after all the teasing in the car. Bobby moans, his fingers clench in my hair and his dick pulses against my tongue as he loses himself to the pleasure. I don’t let him slip out of my mouth until he shoves at my face. “Too much. Please, Martin. No more.”

Someday, I’d love to make him take more. Torture his over-sensitized post-orgasmic nerves until the discomfort goes full circle and turns back to pleasure. Spend hours making him come until he can’t anymore. It’s a hot fantasy, but that isn’t something we’ve discussed, so I relent, swiping a hand over my spit-slick lips.

Bobby flops back onto the bed, breathing hard and rubbing his face with his hands. "God, I needed that. Thanks." Eventually, he peers at me between his fingers. "Did you want me to return the favor when I stop resembling an overcooked noodle?"

I snort at his imagery, my boy limp and spent from his pleasure. He reaches down to deal with the used condom, tying it off and tossing it toward his trash bin. It falls short, but the mess is contained, so that's a problem for later. He doesn't so much as sit up, still recovering.

"Take your time, Bobby boy. How long do we have?"

He props himself up on an elbow to glance over at the clock on the stove. Wow, this place is tiny compared to what I'm used to.

"I don't have anywhere to be until five. So we have a couple more hours." He flashes me a hopeful little smile.

"Perfect," I grin at him, leaning in to brush a gentle kiss to his lips. For a while, we just exchange lazy kisses as he catches his breath.

Then Bobby gets his second wind. He moans and arches against me. It's an unaccustomed thrill to find myself pressed against him in his bed. Bodies entwined and mouths locked together in a passionate kiss as Bobby ruts his naked dick against my thigh while he hardens again.

I haven't come in my pants in a damn long time. Not since Charlie was around to make me do it. I force my thoughts away from the past and focus firmly on the here and now. The sweet young man pliant in my arms as he opens himself to me. His body and his affection laid bare as we kiss. I fumble my dick free, so that I can stroke us both.

"Get us naked first, hot stuff." I soften the order with a kiss to the corner of his mouth. We disentangle to get our remaining clothing out of the way. I pull him on top of me and pick up where we left off. Only now he's sitting astride my hips, our mouths moving together in a kiss as vital as air. Bobby rides me, humping with all the desperate need of a horny twenty-something. God, I could have fun with that kind of stamina.

I wrap my fist around our dicks and his thrusts are pure pleasure as every inch of his slender cock slides along mine. I grab his ass with my free hand, urging him to continue thrusting himself against me whenever he flags. It seems to go on and on, waves of pleasure shared back and forth between us as we fuck my fist.

Our bodies move together as one until he pounds out his release, muscles tensing and quivering. He breaks off the kiss and clings to me through his second orgasm of the evening. Bobby shudders with the aftershocks while I hold him close. I like this part, the comedown from the rush of good sex. And I'm glad we have time to linger on it tonight. He cuddles into me, nestling his head on my chest to rest under my chin.

"Still didn't get you off."

"Hush, I can wait."

He snuggles close for a little longer, soaking in the human contact. I card my fingers through his hair, doing the same. It's nice to connect with him after the fireworks. It's been a while since I let myself have this side of sex. The gentle lingering touches of a lover instead of a quick hard fuck where we each go our own way before the jizz even cools.

Most of the people I play with these days either don't want cuddles as part of their aftercare, or have another partner to snuggle with them once the scene ends. I could ask for it, as something that I need coming down from a scene. Except I never fully realized how much I needed it until now. Subs aren't the only ones who need care after a scene.

Again, not that this was a scene. Or that Bobby is my sub.

Orgasm denial could be a scene, but I hardly denied him for long. If we're going to keep doing this, we ought to have a frank conversation about what we both want and our limits. But it's just a casual fling for now and I don't want to break into his afterglow with serious talk. Tonight can be more of the same. Vanilla with a twist of spice. Just because we both have kinks doesn't mean sex always has to be kinky.

Bobby squirms in my arms and I reluctantly let him go.

"I might have, uh, practiced last night?"

"Practiced?" I ask, drawing a blank as to what he means. The idea of him going out and fucking someone else last night gives me a tightness in my chest that I'm unaccustomed to, though. I thought what we did was good for us both. Did he leave unsatisfied? I rarely misread people that badly.

"Yeah." He fidgets, then reaches into the box of condoms on his nightstand to hold one up. "You said next time that I should put the condom on you with my mouth, so I looked up some videos and tried it. With my toys. So, if you want, I could show you my work?"

"I'd love to see what you can do." I chuckle at his enthusiasm and the relief of knowing that he thought of me last night instead of going out to find someone else. Jeez, possessive much? He isn't mine. But I'd like to see more of him. That interest must be mutual, if he learned a new trick just to impress me.

I prop myself on my elbows to watch him kneel between my knees. He gets out the condom, tucks the tip between his lip and his tongue. He lowers his mouth down my shaft, diving down to the root and rolling the latex into place in one smooth glide that has me pumping deep into his hot mouth. Damn, he's good with his tongue, stimulating me as he lifts back off to grin at me. His expression is expectant, obviously waiting to be praised over his new trick.

"Sexy as fuck, hot stuff. You *have* been practicing, huh? Get back up here and I'll show you how hard that makes me." I pat my thighs and he scrambles back up to straddle my lap, his own cock already at half mast again. We kiss then, with him giving me a writhing, wriggling lap dance that drives me right to the edge of bliss and keeps me there. When I've had enough, I break off the kiss. He's panting like he might be close to the edge again. Damn, one of these days I'm going to push that youthful stamina to the limits. But not today.

"Down. I want to fuck your mouth, hot stuff."

"Yes, please." Bobby slips out of my lap and sucks me off like I'm his favorite treat.

A shiver runs through him when I moan his name as I pump out my release buried halfway down his throat. Bobby doesn't seem as overwrought as he did after last night. I still hold on to him for as long as he lets me. He makes me want things I haven't dared let myself desire in a very long time. A partner who stays longer than a few scenes in the private rooms at Adventures.

CHAPTER 7

Bob

Friday night, I meant to ask Martin if we could plan to meet up again, but I never got around to it. Instead, I ended up running out on Martin when Joel called and woke me from dozing in Martin's arms after round three. We were both scrambling to get dressed and out the door, since his daughter was expecting him home, too.

So I didn't ask for a repeat. I have his number from that first night, but I haven't called. I don't want to act clingy just because he blew my mind in bed. Several times.

Joel and the others gave me shit for being late to our game, but I was too glowy from epic sex to care. When I got home and realized I hadn't made plans to see Martin again, the glow faded. It made me admit to myself that I want more passionate nights with him. And more days of flirting and exchanging meaningful glances that only make me want him more.

So, when Martin walks in to Sin and Chocolate at his usual time on Saturday morning, it's a relief. His presence fills me with giddy anticipation. Guess he couldn't resist coming back for more. We pick up where we left off with the flirting and I convince him to sneak away to the backseat of his car for a quickie on my lunch break. It's all the more thrilling because the garage where he parked is busier in the mid afternoon and I can hear people talking nearby as I swallow around Martin's gorgeous cock.

I spend Sunday pining over him, since I have the day off. I give in to the impulse to text him, and end up jerking off several times to memories of our encounters. Martin lets me know he's got a busy week, but he'll be in on Monday for his coffee fix. So I'll still be seeing him, even though he'll be at the cafe less.

When he shows up during a rare early morning lull in business on Monday morning, I take it as a sign from the universe that I should get up the guts to ask about his services as a DM. If I can afford his rates, that would mean finally getting a regular game going again, without having to DM.

I might even ditch Joel and the others so I can join a new group I get along with better. The more I consider it, the more I like that plan. Plus five bonus points for not having to deal with Joel anymore. We've drifted apart in recent years. Joel looks down on my job even though I'm doing exactly what I want with my life, and unlike him, my job doesn't make me miserable most days. The others may or may not agree with his views, but none of them stand up for me. I don't either.

I guess part of me is holding out for that protector who can vanquish my bullies for me. Someone like Martin. I can picture him telling Joel what to do with his insults in the same no-nonsense tone he told me to suck his dick. The one that makes me want to obey his every command.

"So, you mentioned that you DM?" I blurt the question as I bring Martin's coffee to where he is going over his notes at his usual table. I linger to chat after handing over his drink.

"Right." Martin nods, turning the cup in his hands. "Among other things."

I lick my lips and get to the point. Why is this making me so nervous? Nothing wrong with paying him for a service, right? I guess it's the idea that I should be able to find a friend who wants to do it without having to pay? I don't know, but it's probably silly to be this nervous, except I like Martin and I don't want him to think less of me for any reason. "As in, working as a professional dungeon master?"

"That is what DM generally means in our scene, yes." Martin gives me a wry smile and sips his drink. I stare at the way his throat works when he swallows. Yeah, I've got it bad. All the more reason to get him to run our game, though. That would guarantee me spending more time with Martin. "I facilitate everything that goes on in my little world." Martin adds with a bemused smile, clearly seeing how caught up in him I am.

"Right." I rub my sweaty palms on my thighs. "Sounds perfect. What kind of world are we talking? Typical fantasy?" As though I've played in other campaign settings. My group is so predictable, it's getting old. I guess if I agree to DM for them, I could mix things up. But it's a lot of work that my heart isn't into doing. Not when no one in my group will appreciate anything but the combat.

"Does a typical fantasy exist? Everyone enjoys different aspects of what we do. But in general, I try to offer a little of everything." Martin explains, spreading his hands over the table. I glimpse his meticulous dungeon map. He's got an eye for detail. The map looks almost like a blueprint. Then again, he's renovating his business, so it might not be a map for a game.

"What's your favorite?" I ask. I wipe up an imaginary mess on his table to give myself an excuse to prolong our conversation.

"Well, I'm adding in some hooks for suspension, so that will be a huge feature when we reopen. One that Monty, one of my regulars, has been begging for."

That takes me a minute to parse. Story hooks make sense, but suspension? He must mean suspense. He's got me hooked already, and I don't even know the basics of whatever campaign he's planning on running. "Oh, cool, starting up a whole new narrative?"

"You could say that." Martin sounds puzzled by my wording, though, cocking his head to look at me more closely. "It's going to be a big change when we reopen. I'm making the main room more atmospheric for public play. Plus, we're separating and upgrading the lounge area to have more of a pub vibe, but without the booze. Play and intoxication don't mix well. Not to mention, the licensing process with the province is a hassle."

"Oh yeah, playing drunk or high always sounds like a better idea than it is. Our group had to ban drinking at our sessions a while back after we lost Arty to a series of terrible decisions." I sigh. Arty was a goblin non-player character who our party took in as a sort of mascot. Kel intended him as a throwaway character who brought us messages from our patron. Our party all but goblin-napped him and made him one of us for the better part of our last campaign. Until he died tragically because we were too drunk to notice the ambush waiting for us as we were leaving town.

"My condolences," Martin puts his hand over mine, all solemn, like I lost more than a character that night. It's sweet that he cares, so I don't correct whatever assumptions he's making. "Guess I don't have to explain it to you."

"Nope, I get it. So, what other adventures does your club offer?"

"We have some specialized modules in the private rooms."

"Oh, cool, like what?"

"This and that. The newest addition has an old world vampire aesthetic. We pulled out all the stops with the decor, too. Rich fabric on the walls plays a double role as decoration and sound dampening. A life size coffin for sensory deprivation, a St. Andrews cross. Basically, you can let out your inner vamp. Some of my regulars requested it and it came out pretty cool. We've also got your traditional medieval dungeon cell, among others."

"Sounds outstanding. I'd love to see it sometime. Vamps aren't my thing, but it sounds like you go the extra mile to make it an immersive experience for everyone with all the props and stuff."

"We do." Martin nods. "I pride myself on making my dungeon a place where people can let loose and enjoy themselves."

"Okay, how many players do you usually have?"

"At the club? Or as in play partners? I prefer one-on-one for any scenes I'm personally a part of, but I could do more."

"One-on-one? Huh. That's not what I'm used to. What would that entail?"

"Whatever you like." Martin purrs, leaning back in his seat to watch me better.

"Sounds rather intimate." I fiddle with my cleaning rag, giving up all pretense of working.

"It is. Which is why I don't play with just anyone. But I like you, hot stuff." Martin winks at me. "What do you like?"

"I've always been more interested in the roleplay than the violent parts." I say, caught in his too perceptive gaze. He's watching me with the same intensity from the moment before our first kiss the other night, and I shiver at having his complete focus on me. Like he can strip me bare with only a glance. I keep talking, as though that might offer some sort of protective barrier. "Sometimes it seems like I'm the only one in my group who isn't all about maximizing damage capability."

"You hang out with a bunch of sadists or something?" Something that might be worry furrows Martin's brow. It's sweet that he cares about whether I'm enjoying the game.

"Sometimes it seems like it, yeah." I chuckle, because it's not a big deal. The others would be just as happy with a campaign that's nothing but a bunch of battles strung together on a flimsy pretext. That isn't wrong, but it makes us a poor fit for each other. Another reason I've been longing to find a DM like Theo. Someone who focuses on other aspects of gameplay than combat. Someone like

Martin. "They're all about the beat sticks, you know?"

"And that's not your style?" Martin sympathizes.

"Not really." I shrug, aware that I've been lingering at his table a bit too long for someone delivering a refill and tidying, but unable to tear myself away from him. "Like I said, that part has its place, but I like a little more RP in my fun and games."

"And what role would you like to play, Bobby?" Martin gazes into my eyes like he wants nothing more than to hear my answer.

I shrug, squirming at the nickname because it again reminds me of being on my knees for him, and how much I want a repeat. Heck, I've been with him three times now, and I still want more. All of him. "I've been interested in roleplaying something less mainstream. Like, way out of the box. I've been mulling over using a disaffected executioner who specializes with a single tail? Something along those lines. Our old DM wasn't comfortable with it, though. No one in our group has done anything similar before. He liked to keep things simple, so he worried about balancing everything, if I threw that into the mix."

"I see. Well, he was right that you're better off saving that kind of play for someone who is knowledgeable about the tools and familiar with the damage they can do. I know my way around a whip. If you'd be interested in playing with me sometime." Martin is looking at me like he wants nothing more than to play with me, though possibly more of the sexy games from last week rather than RP. I am *so* down for both sex and roleplay with him.

"That would be great. We can meet up to talk about the details after my shift? I mean, if you aren't too tied up with work stuff?"

Martin chuckles. "I think you'll find it's you getting tied up. But it would be my pleasure to show you around my dungeon and make you scream."

"Oh, so you're one of *those* DMs?" I tease, hand on my hip as I nudge his shoulder playfully. Any excuse to get some contact.

"Always out to make everyone in the party cry mercy?"

"Yep. I can think of nothing better than having you at my mercy, hot stuff." Martin must agree about finding excuses to touch. He catches my wrist before I can pull away and gives my hand a gentle squeeze. Our gazes lock together and there is so much heat there, I can't wait to get him alone again.

"Cool. So, tonight? I'm not sure if I can afford your rates, or a club membership, but I'd like to try?"

"Don't worry about it. We're taping up plastic to try to contain the mess today, to prepare for the demolition, but tonight I can show you the rooms that are available by appointment. And I'll get you a guest pass for the big reopening, if you want to visit and see what we're all about once we are fully open again. Perks of knowing the owner, I can grease the wheels on the membership process as long as your background check comes back clear." He smiles at me and I don't even question why a D&D club would need to do background checks. It's probably a precaution to make sure potential members are serious about joining. Or something.

"That sounds terrific! Thanks, Martin."

"It's my pleasure, Bobby." Martin says it low, soft enough I catch myself leaning in to hear him better. It reminds me of when he told me to come for him and my dick twitches at the memory. Martin is watching me with an amused smile, like he can tell how much he is affecting me. His phone buzzes with a message and he glances at the screen. "Oh, that's my cue to go meet my staff at Adventures, but I'll pick you up after your shift. Text me?"

"Will do! Good luck today."

Martin stands, gathering his belongings to leave. "See you soon, Bobby." He kisses my cheek before he goes. It's the sort of casual affection I wouldn't expect from a hook up, and his nickname for me feels like an endearment. The kind shared between lovers. I guess at some point after you fuck three times and plan to continue screwing at every opportunity, it becomes something more than casual sex. I hope so anyway.

Tonight will be all kinds of fun. The most I've had with roleplay in ages. Martin better not mind fucking at his club. He said it's got private rooms, so I can tell myself that it isn't off the table.

CHAPTER 8

Martin

When we get to Adventures, Bobby cranes his neck to take in everything, eager to explore. He's all smiles in the reception area. His expression turns puzzled when we walk into the common area that we're dividing into the play space and lounge. My crew has prepared the big open room to begin gutting it tomorrow morning, once the dumpster I scheduled arrives.

We stored the furniture that I'm keeping in some of the private rooms. All that remains are some old cabinets, a rickety table, and a couple of big couches that have seen better days. All of which I'm planning to replace. When I open the door to one of the private rooms, careful not to tear the plastic sheeting that we placed over each door, Bob pales considerably.

Bobby clears his throat. "Hey, uh, Martin?"

"Yes?" I tilt my head to watch him better, trying to see the room through his eyes. I brought him into one of the more generic rooms, so it's not like there is anything too extreme lying around. Nothing like the wickedly sharp flechettes one of my regulars likes to use with his long-time partner. Blood play requires extra precautions. We keep that to a single easy to sanitize private room. Along with the medical kink equipment that Doc, a long-time member, donated when he retired from his private medical practice.

Nothing stands out as particularly shocking. Bobby's reaction surprises me. The gear in here is simple. The focal point is an adjustable padded bench with several places to attach restraints. It's good for spankings, or fucking, or any other creative use my patrons might find for it. A cabinet against the wall holds an assortment of easy to clean items for impact play, sanitizing wipes, a few different sizes and styles of cuffs for newbies to try out. Nothing too extreme.

Bob swallows hard. "Um, what kind of club did you say this was?" He bites his lip, eyes darting around the space, like he's trying to fit the pieces together.

"A kink club." A knot of tension is forming in my chest. I thought he knew. We've had so many exchanges that made it seem obvious he realized what kind of club I run. He asked me to whip him earlier today, for goodness' sake. How could he not know?

"Oh. Oh! Fuck." Bobby buries his face in his hands and laughs. Soft at first, so that I'm not sure if he's laughing or crying, I reach for him, concerned, but his laughter gets louder and he looks up at me. "You're—" He cracks up again, trying to catch his breath and holding his belly, "Oh, my god. I..." He shakes his head and tries again. "I can't... oh, shit, Martin, this is too much."

"Glad that amuses you?" I try not to let my apprehension about his response get to me. Is it so ridiculous that I would run a kink club?

"Sorry," he gasps, holding his sides like it hurts to laugh that hard. "Not laughing at you."

I cross my arms and wait for him to explain what he finds so hilarious. Must be a doozy, since he can't seem to stop laughing long enough to catch his breath. Let alone explain it.

"What kind of club did you think it was?" I ask when his laughing subsides enough that he can actually answer.

"D&D. Or like VentureQuest. You know, nerds like me sitting around rolling dice and having adventures?" Bob mimes rolling dice. Oh. Wow, big misunderstanding. It is kind of funny. I chuckle.

"Oh. You assumed I was that kind of DM?" I uncross my arms and try to relax so we can discuss where this all leaves us.

"Yeah. You kept talking about designing dungeons for people and showing everyone a good time, so I figured you meant running campaigns for gaming groups."

"Do they actually have clubs for that?" I try to hide my skepticism.

"Well, I mean, there are a lot of local game stores that have regular groups who play in person. I figured it was like that, only more specialized? And yeah, there are professional DMs who will run games for a group. It can be a lot of work to organize if no one in your group wants to do it." Bob lifts his hands and shrugs.

"Okay. Well, good to know. Now that you mention it, I think a few of the subs at Adventures are into that kind of game. If you hang around the club, I'll introduce you. I guess calling the place Adventures didn't help with the confusion, huh?" I give him a rueful smile, wondering if he's going to walk away now that he knows the truth. I hope not, our sex has been amazing and I want to explore more with him.

"Yeah. Where did that come from, anyway?"

"Charlie. My late wife and I started the club after university. The name was an inside joke. When we first discussed kink, she brought it up by showing me a bunch of kink gear from her personal wish list. I'd never seen most of it before. I asked what it was all about. Charlie gave me her slyest smile and told me it was 'for people who like to get adventurous. In bed.' Then she invited me along to have an adventure with her, to see if I liked it, and I was hooked."

"Okay, that's sweet." Bob reaches out and rubs his hand along my forearm. "I'm sorry you lost her."

"Like I said, she's been gone a long time." It means more than I'd have expected to share that old memory. "I still miss her, but having the club means I get to keep her legacy alive."

"I'm glad. So. I guess this is super awkward, huh? Like, earlier today, I thought we were discussing me paying to have you run a custom D&D campaign for me. Either with a group or solo. But now I'm realizing you heard something completely different?" Bob gestures at the cabinets. "Something that features whatever you've got in there?"

"Yeah. I thought you meant sexy roleplay. With a single tail." I open up the armoire style door and display the neatly arranged ranks of toys. The collection I keep in here for club members to use is simple stuff that is easy to clean between patrons. Most of the regulars bring their own toys anyway, but I provide the basics for newbies to get an idea of what they enjoy. Or if someone forgets their toys at home. Paddles, floggers, canes, and the single tail are all displayed nicely in the cabinet.

I watch Bob's reaction to the array. His eyes dart over each object, finally resting on the whip. I came into tonight thinking I might get to use it with him. Guess that isn't happening. He licks his lips and I get the impression the idea of trying the items on display doesn't turn him off. Quite the opposite. He looks more interested than freaked out or scared and he isn't turning tail, so our misunderstanding could prove to be an opportunity in disguise. Still, whipping him might prove too intense for a first session with a total newbie who may or may not even be into pain play. I set aside the half-formed scene I'd been mulling over to try with him and secure the cabinet doors.

We definitely need to talk things out before doing anything else. I lift an arm toward him, inviting him closer. "Why don't we go to the reception area. Or I can take you home. It was never my intention to spring kink on you. I understand if you need time to process everything."

"No." Bob shakes his head, stepping into my space and letting me settle the offered arm around his shoulders. "I don't want to leave. I still like you. And the sex is fucking fire. If having you tell me what to do and giving me permission and punishments is part of this whole kinky BDSM thing, I guess it's right up my alley. This isn't what I expected, but tell me more."

"If you're into this, then we can talk about what sort of adventures we both might want to explore together." I gesture toward the door. "Right this way. I can answer any questions you have. Though I'm not certain I have much to offer if you need someone to run a campaign for you and your group. Sorry to disappoint."

"It's fine. Talking about it with you, or rather, thinking we had it all hammered out, made the answer clear. I'd rather hire a DM to play the sort of game I enjoy than continue to hope my old group will change to a play style I enjoy more. Or suddenly start respecting me, for that matter."

"Good for you. I'm guessing the guys who stopped by the cafe the other day were there to get you to run a game for their group. Not monitor safety at a sex party like I assumed from what I overheard?"

"Yeah, I wouldn't sleep with any of the people in my group. Wes is alright, but he's still a bit of a bro, so not my type. And Haley is sweet, but I don't really roll that way. I mean, I'm not bi or pan. But it's cool that you are, just so we're clear."

"Glad to hear it." I smile at him, hoping to ease the anxiety that has him babbling. And it's a relief to confirm what I'd already guessed about him taking my being bi in stride. He accepts that it's a part of me. "It takes guts to stand up for yourself. I'm proud of you for not letting those guys push you into doing anything you aren't comfortable with."

"Thanks. I'm proud of me, too. For finally making the call to move on from them. Now I only need to tell them I'm quitting the group. It's been a long time coming. But enough about that. Let's discuss this adventure of ours."

"That would be my pleasure." I steer him back through the damaged public play space and into reception. We drag two chairs over to the check-in computer to pull up some files. I've got several resources that might help him better understand BDSM, kink, and the scene I'm hoping to introduce him to.

It might be just as well that I got so attached before I realized how new he is to all of this, because if I'd gone into this knowing how inexperienced Bobby is with kink, I'd have said I didn't have time to mentor a baby sub with everything else on my plate this summer. But after our handful of encounters and the hungry way he looked at my toys, I've already decided that I'll make time for him. It will be worth it if he's as interested in exploring his kinks as I suspect he is.

CHAPTER 9

Bob

Tonight didn't go at all like I expected. Who knew Martin was some sort of kinky dungeon master? Well, I guess there were clues. It just never occurred to me he wouldn't be exactly the sort of DM I needed rather than some sort of BDSM dom. Then again, maybe he's still the partner I need.

For one, getting up the courage to ask him about DMing for my group proves to myself that I can ask for what I want. That I can go out there and find the sort of gaming group I desire instead of settling for the dysfunctional group I have.

Point two in Martin's favor, whatever his kinks might be, I enjoyed our nights together. In hindsight, the hints at who he is are there when he lets himself go during sex. His take charge attitude and bossy streak were both major turn ons for me. I liked him telling me what to do in the car. He demanded more from me than I'd have been comfortable offering, but not so much that I didn't want to give it.

The game he made of having me jerk off in his passenger seat, where anybody could have seen if not for the bag shielding my privacy, got me hot as fuck. My own hand never got me so spectacularly aroused before. Probably because it was Martin telling me to use it. And his command making me hold onto his frustrating bulky bag, too.

When I let him use my mouth and force me to swallow him down to the root, it felt amazing. I loved letting him thrust all the way in, until his balls rested on my chin. How he held me there, breath caught in my lungs. Yeah. I've jerked off to my memories of that first night in his car an embarrassing number of times, considering it's only been a few days. And I want more of it.

In my fantasies, he gets rougher, holding me in place, cutting off my air with his dick until I'm desperate for a breath I can't take without his permission. I might be premature for someone I met so recently, but I trust Martin. And he never sprang kink on me on purpose. It was always something he asked about first, inviting me to play a game or give him control of the situation. I want nothing more than to give him control tonight, too.

Now that I've gotten a glimpse at how much deeper this rabbit hole can go, I want to glut myself on Martin and everything he offers me. Because he gave me exactly what I didn't realize I needed, with none of the elaborate props he showed me in that little private dungeon of his. I can only imagine how much more intense our sex life might be with all the tools at his disposal in his own domain.

"Are you listening, Bobby?" Martin frowns at me over the list of kinks that he printed out once we got back to the reception desk.

"Um, no?" I wet my lips. The stern set of his jaw sends a delicious shiver of anticipation along my spine. Wasn't discipline on the list? What would that entail?

I get lost in a fantasy where he turns me over his knee for a spanking. Do I really want that? God, those thighs of his, yes, I want to feel them flex and tense under my belly while he fondles my ass, or spanks it. Or, frankly, does whatever he wants with me.

I'm pretty sure I'd like anything Martin did to me. Maybe. Some of the stuff in his cabinet looked like it could do serious damage. I have no desire for him to make me bleed. I enjoyed the one spanking I got from a past hookup, though, so it stands to reason the other stuff listed near it would be just as exciting.

Martin snaps his fingers to get my wandering attention back on him before I can go much further into that daydream. When I meet Martin's gaze, shamefaced at my woolgathering, he's fighting a smile, trying to look serious. "Care to share what has your dick so interested and your ears turned off?"

"You." I bat my eyes at him.

"Anything specific about me?" he presses for an answer. That suppressed smile is still tugging at the corner of his lips.

"Yeah. I was thinking if we were into that discipline stuff you mentioned, you could spank me for not paying attention." I fiddle with the edge of the page to occupy my hands.

"Yes, I could." Martin nods. "Is that something you would want?"

"It might be? I've never considered it. But I liked you telling me what to do. With that game the other night? The idea of a punishment makes me hard. And doing things I'm not totally comfortable with because you told me to sounds good. Is it weird that I've done a lot of the things on the list, but never considered them particularly kinky?"

"I'm not one for calling anyone weird, hot stuff. If it makes you happy, and everyone involved is a consenting adult, then I'm not here to yuck in your yum."

"Even if most people consider it gross?" I stare down at the list. There are so many options. Some I've tried, or fantasized about trying, and some scare me. The idea of actually being whipped is terrifying. It seems more extreme than the other stuff listed under impact play.

Some options scare me because I want them. Like fisting and watersports. Will he think less of me for liking it when my ex asked to pee on me? Because I'd enjoyed it and he hadn't. It grossed him out that I got hard.

In hindsight, I guess he wanted to humiliate me, and it had worked. Not because I was ashamed of my reaction. There wouldn't be so much porn featuring piss play if I was the only one who liked it. It was more that I was ashamed that he asked to see that raw, unshielded side of me, and when I gave him what he asked for, he rejected it. Rejected me. I doubt Martin would do that.

If Martin asks me for that level of vulnerability, I believe he'd appreciate what a gift it is to share that with another person. The way he held me after our previous times together says he values what I have to offer. Not just a mutual sexual release, he appreciates me giving him control as much as I crave having him take it.

"Even then. I won't judge you, Bobby."

"I like golden showers. And I enjoy having you tell me what to do in bed. More than what you've already done. Maybe even enforcing that I need permission to come by using chastity devices. Although, not all the time." I skim over the list to be sure I'm hitting all the highlights, listing off what I like and dislike for him until I get to the part with the whips. "I'm not sure about all the different types of pain play listed here, except spanking. I enjoy that. So similar things are probably fine?"

"Are you asking me or telling me?" Martin raises a brow at me.

"Asking? I don't have a good frame of reference for this. From what I understand you can do serious damage with a whip. 1d4 slashing damage might not be much in melee, but it sure isn't something I'd normally equate with sexy times. Like I don't want to be flayed alive. It's something I might want to try, but also it makes me nervous. You said you know what you're doing, so it's something we could work up to trying?"

"1D4? Is that from D&D?" he asks.

"Yeah, it's just how much damage whips do in combat. So, yeah, not a ton, but still more than sounds fun." I fiddle with the list to occupy my hands.

"Whips are a soft limit?" Martin suggests.

"Yes." I nod.

"How do you feel about other types of impact play? Spanking, paddles, riding crops, and floggers?"

"All of that seems okay. Except not the crop? I've watched videos with those and I don't want welts. At least, not tonight. But I mean, if we're doing the RP I wanted to try, hitting me sort of fits the scene, right?"

"That doesn't mean you have to agree to it. There are other things we could do. I can be creative, hot stuff."

"No, I want to try it. You'll stop if I don't like it, right?"

"Always. The minute you say your safe word, the scene stops."

"Okay. Paddle, flogger, and your hand all interest me."

"And bondage is...?"

"Also good." I nod like a bobblehead. "That all sounds good. Oh, and sounding, I saw some videos of that and it looked like something I'd love to try. With or without being tied up."

"Somehow, I'm not surprised you watch a lot of interesting porn." Martin caresses my thigh, so the tease comes off sounding affectionate.

"You don't seem to mind my libido, handsome." I tease him right back.

"That is very true. What about suspension bondage?"

I laugh, remembering our earlier conversation. "Oh my god, you realize I figured you meant suspense. Like leaving a game session on a cliffhanger? But you meant dangling me in the air to have your wicked way with me. Would you fuck me while I'm hanging from these hooks of yours?"

"If that's what you want. Not actual hooks though, the kind that go through your skin. That's a thing, but it's a bit too edge for the club. Once we've got the new gear installed, I would be more than happy to play with other forms of suspension with you. I'm not a rope top. But I think we have a sex swing around here somewhere. Or if you want to get tied up in elaborate and artistic displays, I have friends who can accommodate."

"Oh. Would they want to fuck me?" I try to hide my disappointment at the thought of him sharing me with his friends.

"Some might. If that's what you want? Or it can strictly be about the tying." He sounds hesitant, lips pursed like he dislikes the idea of me fucking anyone else too. That gives me hope.

"I'd have to consider that. I guess I thought..."

"What?"

"I thought this was like a contract? Like we'd only, uh, *play*—is that what you call this—with each other? I don't know, is that totally offensive? Or is this a casual hook up and I'm being clingy?"

"Play or scene both work. You aren't being clingy. It is *always* okay for you to ask me for what you want, Bobby. This isn't a contract. It's just a checklist. A tool to help us discuss each other's preferences and limits and assess our compatibility."

"Right. So. I showed you mine?" I give him a hopeful look, ready to have the focus of all this openness off of me for a minute.

"You want to hear what I enjoy?" Martin leans back in his seat and steeples his fingers over the list.

"Yeah."

"I'm a switch. So, depending on my mood, I sometimes take the role of dominant and sometimes the more submissive role. I enjoy bondage, as a top and a bottom. My skills with rope are adequate to tie you to the bed, but I wouldn't trust myself with suspension work. Unless we used a harness or something. Fucking you in a sex swing is definitely workable if you want me to take you while you're dangling and helpless. I enjoy wielding floggers, or a single tail with a bottom who enjoys the pain. I can do humiliation play with a sub I know well enough to trust them to safe word before any lines get crossed. But it's a bit of a soft limit for me. Watersports aren't something I've done much of. I'm willing to do that kind of scene with you, if you want it. And if you're into sexual roleplay as well as gaming, that's something I'm interested in exploring more, within limits. Some scenes I won't do, but the one you described when we spoke earlier sounded hot."

"Like, executioner and prisoner?" I fight the urge to cringe, remembering how frankly I'd put that out there earlier. Martin wasn't ashamed to discuss it, and I don't want to be either. But, much as I want to share his chill, it's outside my comfort zone to have a casual chat about sexual fantasies beyond dirty talk in private. "Oh my god, you didn't even bat an eye when I told you I wanted that, right in the middle of my work. Geez. You really aren't judging me?"

"I'm really not. Would you still want to try it?"

"Not with the big scary whip. I'm a wimp. We could try it with whatever starter impact toy you judge wouldn't freak me out instead?"

"That's fine. I've got a few gentler paddles and floggers we could try to see what you enjoy. Do you have any medical conditions or physical restrictions I should know about? Heart conditions, allergies, blood-borne pathogens?"

"No, nothing like that. I get tested pretty regularly and I'm negative as of my last check."

"Me too. But at the club, the rule is to use condoms for any penetrative sex. That includes oral and toys."

“Ok. Does that mean we could eventually consider ditching condoms for sex outside the club?” I venture to ask.

Martin hesitates. “That’s not something I do for casual partners.”

“Oh. Right. Sorry, I didn’t mean to imply…”

“Would you be interested in an exclusive relationship, Bobby?” he asks.

“With you?” It’s only been a few days, but damn, he’s got me craving more of him. And technically, this is our fourth date. For a definition of dating that equates to getting up close and personal with each other’s dicks. Still, I like him and nothing ventured, nothing gained.

“That’s the idea, yeah.” He cracks a smile.

“Yes. I mean, I’m not saying I’m ready to commit to forever, or even going bare right away. Just that I like you and if we’re baring our souls and talking about all this intimate stuff that we plan to do together, that’s something I want, too. Not only a dom who ties me up, bosses me around, and makes me come harder than I’ve ever come before in my life. But also, an exclusive boyfriend who fucks me raw. So I can feel his cum leaking out of my ass and know I’m his and he’s mine, and he wants to claim me like that. In ways no one else gets to have me.”

“Damn, hot stuff,” Martin reaches for me and I lean in to the touch as his fingers trace my lips. “Listen to that filthy mouth of yours. I am not opposed to dating you. Or fucking you without a condom when we aren’t at Adventures. On the condition that you aren’t doing that with anyone else, and we both get tested beforehand.”

“Okay. If we’re dating, does that mean no sex with other people?” I check, giddy with the anticipation of getting more time with Martin.

"It can. Is that what you want?" Martin tips his head questioningly.

"Yeah." I nod. "Monogamy suits me." I squirm in my seat, hyperaware that I might come on too strong. I don't want him to think I'm too needy. We only met a week ago, but he's already consuming my thoughts in that way new relationships always seem to do. Maybe it's just the lure of really good sex, but I think there could be something more here. Something I need in a partner. Even though we've only shared a few brief hook ups, I don't want to be with anyone else. Not until I've explored this with Martin. "I feel weird asking for this so fast, but, I've enjoyed being with you."

"Relax, Bobby." He cups my cheek, and I lean into the touch. "I'm glad you're asking for what you want. I like you too. It's fine if you don't want to sleep with other people. I don't either, not when I'd only be comparing them to you. We can be exclusive when it comes to sex. Sure it's fast, but if we're both happy, who cares? How do you feel about doing scenes with other people?"

"You mean all this kinky stuff? Like would it be okay for someone else to tie me up? Or for you to use your whips on someone else?"

"Yes, that's what I mean."

My knee-jerk reaction is that I want him to myself. But then I consider what he said about helping me find people to try things with that he isn't comfortable doing. Like suspension. It makes me appreciate that we don't have to be everything to each other. It's obvious from talking to him that Martin adored Charlie, and he says they did kinky play with other people. So if I agree to this, I can have my exclusive boyfriend and still agree to us both indulging in our kinks with others as long as we check in about it first.

I'm looking forward to exploring what we both enjoy together, but it might be nice to try things with other people, too. As long as it's about enjoying a shared kink and not about sex or being emotionally intimate with someone else beyond the bounds of friendship. "I'm not sure how I'd feel about sharing that part of you? I don't want to be the one calling the shots. So if you need to submit, or whatever, I am fine with you having that need met with someone else. If you want to do things that aren't sexual with other people, I'm open to seeing how it goes? I might want to watch? To be honest, this is all new. I'm not sure."

"That's fine. We can see how it goes. How about, for now, if either of us wants to scene with someone else, we agree to keep it non-sexual and run it by the other person first?"

"Okay. That works for me."

"I'll also need you to read over and sign the club's release forms. And we need an NDA on file that you promise not to share anything you see here with the public. Some of our members have privacy concerns. If word got to the wrong people, it could damage their careers or other aspects of their lives. So we require everyone to sign." He turns to rifle through a filing cabinet and retrieves the forms in question.

"That's not at all intimidating." I swallow hard, anxious and overwhelmed at the bald statement of risk.

"It's about consent. You can't give informed consent if you don't understand the risks you're agreeing to. And the NDA is to protect all our members' privacy as best we can. There is a section at the top outlining the risks you're taking on as a sub. If the club or your dom does something reckless that endangers you outside of what you might reasonably expect, this waiver won't stop you from pursuing damages. It's meant to protect us if something goes wrong that's outside our control and make sure you know what you are signing up for. You don't have to sign anything you aren't comfortable with, though. Read through and see what you think." Martin hands me the paperwork.

“Okay, thanks.” I take the papers without looking at them yet. “Bringing in liability and an NDA makes this seem scarier.”

“I get that. What we do can be intimidating. Especially if you aren’t used to it. I understand the amount of trust you’d be placing in me if you decide to try more of the things on our list. Charlie was my Domme and being her submissive pushed me in ways I never would have imagined. She helped me grow, in every aspect of my life. Since her passing, I’ve been more interested in the dom role. But I still understand first hand the trust you’d be putting in me by offering your submission.”

I take a deep breath and nod.

Martin covers my hand with his before I can scribble a hasty signature on the line for guests and new members. “Take your time to consider. The offer to try this out won’t expire because you need a few days to mull it over. This is a lot to process. If you want me to take you home to sleep on it, I will. We don’t have to do anything tonight.” His focus as I meet his gaze pins me in place. I don’t back down though. I want this.

“No, I don’t need to sleep on it. I never considered myself kinky, but like I said, nothing on that list shocks me. And plenty of what we discussed are things I’ve already tried. With people who didn’t inspire half as much confidence in their ability to deliver on their promises of a good time as you.”

Martin searches my face. His palm is a warm restraint on the back of my hand, preventing me from signing anything in haste. I’m not sure what he’s looking for. Signs of doubt? He must not find them, because he nods and pats my hand before releasing his grip on it. “I’ll leave you alone to read over everything. You can back out at any point. And we use a stoplight system for safe words at the club. Red for stop the scene right now, yellow for slow down or discuss a concern, and green for keep going. It keeps things consistent for our DMs to know what to listen out for when they are monitoring scenes.”

"Okay. That seems easy enough to remember. Can we still try a scene, or whatever you call it, tonight? Or did I ruin the mood by making us talk about all this?"

"Talking about what we both want and expect isn't a mood killer. You telling me all your fantasies is a turn on for me. I'd love to take you back into the private room, put you in cuffs and play with that tight ass of yours. Is that still something you want?"

"Yes. And the medieval torturer RP?" I check.

"We can include a bit of that, too, if it's what you want. Would that include you begging for it all to stop?" Martin arches a brow in question. Why does that sound so incredibly hot? I mean, if it were an actual situation it would be the furthest thing from sexy, but with him, as a game? I like the idea.

"Yeah. Probably. If I want to stop, I say red, right?" I force a nervous smile. Butterflies seem to have taken wing in my stomach at the possibility I might try some of the things on that list tonight. With Martin.

"Right." He nods. "And I want you to use the safe words to communicate with me. I'll never be mad about you telling me you need a break or something hurts in a bad way, or you have to pee. Or anything else that isn't working for you. We have to trust each other, okay?"

"Okay. Let's see how it goes. I want to try this, Martin. I enjoy playing sexy games with you."

"Alright. If you don't have more questions, I'll give you a minute to go over all the paperwork while I get set up. And when I come back, you can still decide this isn't for you, okay? I won't hold it against you."

"Okay."

"Great, then I'm off to prepare the torture chamber." Martin stands to go, bending to kiss my brow on his way past me. He claps me on the shoulder before he goes back into the club. I stare after him, uncertain any of this is real, but more than eager to try it all.

When I suggested the idea for a character, this was far from the context I'd intended. But discussing Martin playing the role of a whip wielding punisher right out of one of my D&D campaigns has me all kinds of hot and bothered. Maybe that's weird, but heck if I can bring myself to care. Martin has shown me he's worthy of my trust in all the little details.

He made sure we used condoms, even when I was so turned on I was ready to risk sucking him off without one. Oral without a condom isn't exactly foreign to me, but it's endearing that he cared enough to look out for me by using one. He took care of me when I let him skull fuck me.

He's the first person who held me when I got all shaky after sex. No intrusive questions, just reassurances while I came down from the rush of my orgasm and being bossed around. He even tried to make sure I wasn't alone when he had to leave. And despite his tendency to take charge, he has always made sure that it's what I wanted beforehand. I believe he'll take care of me in this, too.

I read over the documents and sign up to try all the kinky sex Martin wants to throw at me. Guess I'm ready for him to give me that adventure after all.

CHAPTER 10

Bob

When Martin comes back from preparing the room, he's no longer wearing his usual business attire. I'm not sure where he was keeping the skin-tight pants he replaced them with, but they sure leave little to the imagination. Damn, I want to get him back in my mouth. And other places.

Martin waits in the doorway for me to finish staring at his dick bulge. I tear my eyes away and peruse his broad bare chest; it reminds me of being pinned against him while we frotted the other night, then held close to him after we came.

I like his chest. Martin crosses his arms over it, obscuring my view and prompting me to glance up at his face. He's giving me this knowing grin, like he can tell exactly what I'm thinking. Well, I couldn't be more obvious, drooling all over him.

"You, uh, look good."

"Right back at you." Martin runs his eyes over the black attire I wore to work. It's nothing special, so I shrug. "What did you decide?"

"Same thing I decided when we talked earlier. Let's do this. The whole roleplay thing, and I want you to fuck me after."

His gaze flickers toward the papers.

"Yeah, I signed your release forms. I understand there are risks involved in letting a guy tie me up and spank me. Or other stuff. I'm cool with it. I trust you to take care of me."

"And you remember your safe words?"

"Red, yellow, and green. Can we do this?" I can't help the eagerness. All this talking about sex with him has me more than ready to actually do it.

"Ah, so now you're going to top from the bottom?" Martin raises his eyebrow at me.

"Huh?"

"Bossing me around, even though you asked me to control the scene." He sounds amused, despite the rebuke in his words.

"Um. Sorry?"

"It's fine." Martin's grin turns devilish as he pushes away from the doorframe. "You're supposed to be my prisoner, it's to be expected that you'd ask for all kinds of things I'm not going to give you." He steps into the room, advancing on me.

Oh shit, I like this. More than I expected to. I stand, retreating until I fetch up against the reception counter.

Martin casually pulls a pair of handcuffs out of a drawer, holding them up to show me. I nod, even though the idea of him closing those around my wrists makes everything seem so much more real. Martin crowds me up against the counter. I grind against him, which gets a startled snort of amusement out of him.

"The king warned me against your wiles, spy. I'm here to question you." Martin manhandles me around, bending me over the desk until my cheek presses against my paperwork. He pulls my hands behind my back. I struggle, but it's a pretty feeble effort, just enough to prompt him to push me down more firmly. It gives me a great excuse to rub my ass against his erection, and he leans into it, as turned on by our game as I am, thank god.

I like the idea of playing a spy trying to seduce my captor. The latter part of that role won't take much effort to play, considering how turned on Martin has me. He seems comfortable slipping into a role, too, but I guess that shouldn't surprise me. He's had plenty of practice with all manner of sexual games. Practice I'm reaping the rewards of. Score.

"The more you fight it, the harder it will go for you," Martin warns, snapping the first cuff closed.

I take that as Martin encouraging me to struggle, so I squirm and try to tug my arm free. "No, let me go!"

He handles my resistance with ease, forcing the second cuff around my wrist and grinding against my ass again. "Color?" He asks as I rub myself against him, utterly shameless with my desire.

"Green."

"Good, tell me if that changes." Martin breaks character to kiss the back of my neck before stepping away. I straighten up as soon as his weight is no longer pressing me down. "Come along and be an obedient prisoner."

Well, that's my cue to attempt escape. I try to wrench my hands free so I can make a break for it.

Martin still has hold of the cuffs, and he lifts my wrists upward, barely exerting any force. He doesn't have to. With my hands bound behind me, all it takes to subdue me is pulling them out and up a few centimeters until the strain aches in my shoulders. "None of that. It would be child's play to dislocate your shoulders like this. Be a good boy for me," Martin chides.

His words could be a threat from his character to mine, but they double as a gentle warning for me not to hurt myself for real. That warms me to my toes. Martin is taking every part of this seriously, giving me something I've never acknowledged that

I wanted before him. And he's doing it by engaging in my interests, combining my love of fantasy games with his kinks. Or possibly *our* kinks, considering how much I enjoyed the tamer version of his games that we've already played. It means more to me than I can express that this caring, successful protector of a guy could want to make me happy.

I let him march me through the big open room and back to one of the private rooms. This one looks like it could be a castle dungeon. A stonework facade with rings bolted into it at various spots along the far wall. Furniture I can't name stands beside a rack of torture implements.

Martin guides me to the wall, pressing me against it with my back to the room. He unfastens one of my cuffs, swiftly lifting my still bound wrist to fasten it to a chain dangling above my head. My temporary freedom barely registers before I'm secured to the wall. Martin recaptures my free wrist and fastens it next to the other.

"There. Now we can get these clothes out of the way." Martin gives my ass a smack, then tugs at the waistband. My character might fight him or protest, but I wiggle my hips to help him get the pesky clothing out of the way as fast as possible. Martin suppresses a laugh. "Such a horny little spy, aren't you? Was the king wrong and you really aren't a spy? Are you a naughty boy in need of a spanking for poking your nose where you have no business being?"

"Yes. That's it. I work in the kitchens. It was my turn to deliver a meal to the prince when the guards caught me in his rooms. I swear, I only wanted to feed the prince his dinner. I'm no spy."

"And that's why you were lurking about in his dressing room?" Martin squeezes my bare ass cheek.

I moan and press into his hand. He pulls away and gives me a single sharp crack of his open palm against each cheek that makes me gasp and my dick throb with need. Fuck, yeah, this whole scenario is making me as hard as I've ever been. I might be into restraints. And spanking, but I already knew that. Both sensations combined magnifies my enjoyment. "Maybe I wanted to feed him more than his food," I taunt, thrusting against the wall to get the lewd message across.

Martin gives me several more hard slaps, alternating sides before rubbing both cheeks hard, squeezing and sending more flares of pain through the hot flesh. I squirm, tugging at the chains, unable to hold still.

"Propositioning the prince? That's an interesting defense, little spy." Martin steps away and I turn my head to see what he's doing. "Do you expect me to believe you?"

"It's the truth, and you're nothing but a brute," I reply, twisting around more, since he isn't there to stop me.

Martin returns, mashing my chest against the wall without a word. "Looks like you need more incentive to tell the truth." He kicks my feet apart and fastens them to two cuffs set a bit more than shoulder width apart. Once I'm secured, he reaches between my legs to stroke me. "Color?"

"Green."

"Now, tell me who sent you?"

"No one, I just wanted to fuck a prince." I taunt, bracing for the blow I know to expect for my defiance.

"Try again. Who sent you to poison the prince?" Martin punctuates the question with something new. This time, the hard crack against my ass isn't his bare palm. It's something unyielding, and the impact seems to light up my entire ass cheek like it's on fire for a second before it fades to a dull ache. I gasp and flail against my restraints, unsure how to process the more intense sensation or whether I like it. Martin rubs his palm over the site of impact, his warmth keeping every nerve ending at attention.

"Too much?" he asks.

"No." I shake my head. "I'm not talking."

"How much more can you take?" Martin swats my other cheek. Again, the burst of pain floors me. I still haven't decided if I entirely enjoy it. But I'm not ready to throw in the towel either.

"As much as you can dish out," I taunt him, my shaky voice belying my bravado.

"We'll see about that." Martin gives me three more measured smacks on each cheek, hitting a fresh spot each time until my entire ass burns. Even though the final blows aren't as hard as the first one, it hurts. But it also makes my groin ache with the need to come. Especially when Martin steps in close and I can feel how hard he is, his bulge pressing between my aching cheeks. I moan and push back against him.

"Please?" I tip my head back to get a look at him. The need to see him, and connect with my lover behind the role of torturer, grips me and squeezes like a vise. Martin leans in close, letting me meet his gaze, giving me a second to catch my breath as he grinds against me. I lean into him, despite the burn of friction on tender flesh. I moan, falling back into the role, reassured that Martin won't push me too far.

"Tell me who sent you." Martin fists a hand in my hair, wrenching my head back to growl into my ear. His low voice, demanding and edged with cruelty, sends a shiver down my spine.

"Death to tyrants." I might as well be a freedom fighting assassin spy if I'm going to be tortured for my imaginary crimes.

"The only tyrant here is the one who sent you to kill our rightful heir." Martin's breath is hot against my ear. "It's a pity the rebel scum sent you to die for their cause. You failed, by the way. The prince yet lives."

"I volunteered for this mission. No one sent me and I regret only that I failed."

"Well, when I'm through with you, you may come to regret much more than that." Martin reaches around to jerk my dick. I buck into his rough grip, riding back into Martin's pronounced bulge. I'm caught between the pleasure of being stroked and the heat of lingering pain from the paddling he just gave me.

"Think you can take more, spy? Or are you ready to sing about the rebel camp?"

Can I? I'm not sure. The pleasure and pain jumble together until I don't know if I want more or for it to end.

"Do your worst," I taunt. "I'll never talk."

"Don't be so sure." Martin steps away. I miss the warmth of his presence and his soothing touch.

I hear him set the paddle down. Good. That part must be over. I close my eyes and press my forehead against the cool stone facade.

So it startles me half out of my skin when something tickles my bare legs. Several soft strands of what might be leather slide up my thigh, over the curve of my ass, and along my lower back.

"You'll be lashed before the court for your treason. This is a flogger, and its bite will pale compared to what's in store for you." He twitches the implement so that its trailing fingers thud into my shoulder at low speed. Then Martin drags them across my back. The ends tickle my sides as he uses them to give me an ominous caress. A promise of what's coming. "We'll soon see how brave you are when I flay you open in front of a jeering crowd, my little would-be-assassin."

Oh fuck, the suggestion that we could do something like this in front of an audience has me humping the wall again, despite the gruesome imagery. I jerk at my restraints, groaning an inarticulate plea.

"Color?"

"Green. So fucking green."

"You like the idea of being watched, hot stuff?" Martin breaks character, reaching in front of me to drag the ends of the flogger over my straining erection.

"Fuck. Yes." I'm too caught up in trying to anticipate his next move to fuss over Martin stepping out of his role.

"Good." He pulls the flogger away and I'm left leaning against the wall, panting for breath, half braced for whatever Martin does next.

I have no idea what sensations the new toy is going to inflict when he wields it to cause pain. A low whoosh as it cuts the air is my only warning before my shoulders are stinging under the first impact. I cry out, clutch at my chains, arch, trying to escape the next impact that lands cross-hatching the first.

"Ow." I whine.

"Color?" Martin checks in with me.

"Lime?" I hiss through my teeth, still arching away from that last blow.

Martin steps in close, moving into my line of sight. "That isn't a proper answer, Bobby. Talk to me."

"It's, uh, more intense."

"Too intense?" He caresses my cheek, and I nuzzle into his hand, taking comfort in his touch.

"No." I shake my head.

"Do you want to keep going or call the torture part of the night finished?"

"I can take a little more." I'm not sure why I ask to keep going. A need to prove myself? Or is there a part of me that enjoys letting him push me right to the edge of my endurance? Whatever the reasons, I know as soon as I say it that I don't want this to be over. Not yet. "Keep going."

"That's my mouthy little spy." Martin pats my cheek. "You're going to take whatever I want to give you, aren't you, rebel?"

"Yes."

Martin lets the flogger fall across my upper back again. I moan through the pain. The flogger falls again and again. Each strike seems to awaken more nerve endings. Each of them screaming that they've had enough, but it all seems to blend with the pulsing desire that grows with every moment we play at this game. I can't seem to separate the mounting desire for release from the sensations Martin is coaxing from my body. It's something akin to magic, the way his flogger kisses my skin like a lover's caress.

Martin moves from my shoulders to the backs of my thighs, avoiding my lower back. Each thwack of the tails against my ass and thighs awakens fresh pain. The blows make time spool out into a meaningless blur until I lose all track of how long has passed.

The flogger falls across my already sore ass and reignites the fire there. I jerk against my ankle restraints. My cry forms a garbled version of his name. My desperation to have him take me ward with my urgent need for the flogging to be over. I hope Martin thinks I did a satisfactory job in my role, as good as him. He gave me everything I asked for and I want to give him the same in return.

The crinkle of the condom wrapper is music to my ears. Martin's touch is cool as he parts my ass, fingers slick with lube. He pushes them inside, the gentle, relentless pressure coaxing my body to unclench after the tension of waiting for another blow. He withdraws his fingers far too soon and I whine.

"Come back, I need you, please, Martin?"

"Need me to fill you up with my dick, Bobby?"

"Yes. Please. Fuck me."

Martin's cock nudges against my rim. He eases inside of me. I push back against him, accommodating him as best I can with the restraints still holding me in place. When he bottoms out, his hips flush with my sore ass cheeks, it burns all over again. But then he slides most of the way out, wraps his fist around my shaft, and finds the perfect angle to drive his dick inside me. Every inch of him seems to caress my sweet spot.

"God, right there. Right there, Martin. Can't stop. Don't you dare stop… let me come?" I cling to the chain connecting my wrists because I don't think I can keep myself upright with the amount of pleasure zinging through me.

Martin gives me no quarter, driving himself into me as each thrust builds on the last. I am utterly intoxicated by him. Martin consumes my senses. His breath is hot on my back, his dick thrusting into me, driving my pleasure to a crescendo as he claims what's his.

Some strange alchemy seems to transmute the pain from every strike he landed on my ass into this delicious warmth. That liquid heat spreads to coat my entire groin in an ecstasy that rivals anything I've ever experienced before.

Martin stroking me is too much to bear. I can't hold back the orgasm that threatens to thunder through me and wring out every drop of pleasure. Martin keeps up a punishing pace, thrusting into me hard and fast. My knees are already like jelly.

"I can't take anymore, please," I beg.

"Then come for me, my little rebel spy." Martin's voice, tender as he calls me his, is the touch that topples me over the edge into bliss. His powerful arms hold me upright as I buck out the throes of passion, riding him hard. My ass clenches tight around him even as he drives in as deep as he can get. Martin's punishing thrusts joining us together and drawing out the moment as he tips over the edge with me.

Afterward, I'm a little dazed as he rubs some sort of soothing balm into my sorest spots. Martin releases the cuffs and leads me over to a couch in a corner of the public play area. Martin talks me through what he's doing, but my head is all floaty and strange, so I can only seem to nod along. He lowers me gingerly onto a soft blanket covering the cushions, then sits next to me. Martin wraps us both in a cozy blanket, murmuring sweet nothings about how good I was for him.

"You did beautifully. Bobby, thank you for a wonderful scene." Martin kisses my brow. The tender sweetness overwhelms me.

"Thanks." I croak, trembling with the familiar adrenaline crash, but multiplied by a hundred. I'm not sure if I'm thanking him for the compliment, holding me now, or smacking my ass and fucking me silly. Probably all of the above.

I lean over, taking most of my weight off my sore ass cheeks, and bury my face in his chest. Martin holds me as I shiver. He doesn't seem to be in any hurry to rush me out the door or make me talk. Which is ideal, because I'm too scattered to string together anything coherent about the incredible thing we just did. And I'm not entirely certain I could walk out of here right now. Between the lingering aches and being weak at the knees and wrung out from all the various sensations he gave me, I'm spent.

The only thing he urges me to do is sip some water from a straw. It slides down my throat like a cooling balm, so I drink most of the bottle before he sets it aside. Martin wraps me more firmly in the blanket. This is nice, having him fuss over me and hold me rivals the sex for how much I crave it.

I don't have words to describe what's going on in my heart, but a trembling need for Martin to never let me go consumes me. He obliges. His arms around me are like a promise that I can fall apart and he'll be there to hold me together until I don't need him to.

It should terrify me to depend on him this much after sex. To know that he can turn me into a puddle of pleading mush with so little effort, but it's more exhilarating than anything else. I can't articulate how what we did makes me feel. All I know is that Martin is seriously fun to role play with and I want more of this. More of him.

CHAPTER 11

Martin

Bobby falling asleep on my chest after our scene is exactly what I need to ground myself. His steady breathing lulls me. I enjoy taking care of him. Petting him is soothing after giving him his first taste of pain play in my dungeon.

I smile, remembering the cheeky way Bobby took to the role of captured spy. That sort of roleplay isn't my usual style, it often seems like too much when I've watched others play out similar scenes. Superfluous window dressing. But Bobby got so into it that his enthusiasm made playing that way seem natural. A fun added layer. Something to enhance both the impact play and the sex.

It didn't hurt that he was so obviously into the role, and that acting made it easier for him to take what I dished out to him. I could have pushed Bobby further, brought him from defiant bravado to desperate, begging for it to stop. But that was not the scene either of us needed.

My hot stuff needed the confidence boost of daring me to give him more, and showing us both that he could take it. All of it. He probably could have taken more, but I've never been the sort who needs to explore a partner's limits in every scene.

Sometimes it's enough to play with something we both enjoy. And I can say with confidence that we both enjoyed that scene. I'd love nothing more than to stay wrapped up with him all night, if I didn't have other responsibilities. My phone buzzes from where I left it on the side table before we started, along with bottles of cold water and the blanket. I can just reach it without disturbing Bobby's rest.

"Hello?" I answer.

"Hey, Daddy," Tabby says in her sweetest voice. The one that means she either wants something or she's about to tell me something I won't want to hear.

"What's up, Tabby Cat?"

"Nothing. But since you said you'd be out late tonight with your date, I figured I could make some plans, too. Kelsey invited me out to that new club for her birthday and I was hoping I could borrow some cash for drinks and cab fare?"

I resist the urge to get overprotective. She's nineteen, legally old enough to drink with her friends if she wants. It's not like she even had to tell me who she was going with and where they're going, but she did because she knows I worry about her. "Thanks for checking in first. Take some cash and make sure your friends have cab money too, yeah?"

"Yes, Daddy, none of us are driving. Promise. I'll see you in the morning?"

"Yes. Be safe." It's a habit to say it, but I know my kid and she's not one for taking silly risks. Never has been. She's never hung around with a crowd that encourages risky behavior.

Tabby has her mom's practical streak. Even when her school held her back a year because she was struggling after her mother's death, Tabby took the repeated year in stride. No, my girl wouldn't do anything to put her dance career on the line.

"Always, bye." Tabby hangs up on me and I cling to Bob a little tighter, wondering what my daughter would make of my much younger lover. I don't think our relationship will bother her. If this lasts long enough to introduce the two of them, she'll probably be relieved that I'm not alone when she goes gallivanting off to chase her dreams.

I'm confident that they'll get along fine. Bob is a people person at work, always finding some common ground with his customers to draw them into conversation while he makes their drinks. I've spent far too much time watching him instead of doing my work.

It's not just the endorphins from fucking him. I like Bob. I hope he meant what he said about sticking around. That we can remain partners for more than a scene. It's been a long time since I had a partner outside of the bedroom, or more accurately, the club. I miss it.

Bobby stirs in my arms, mumbling something sleepy. "Hmm?"

"Nothing, hot stuff. Rest for as long as you want." I encourage him. And he does for a while longer. At some point, I doze off, still holding him.

CHAPTER 12

Bob

The rest of the week after our first official scene at Adventures, Martin keeps coming into the cafe each morning for his coffee. But he gets super busy with the renovation. I don't see as much of him each day, now that he's no longer commandeering the corner table for work.

That doesn't stop me from fantasizing about doing more adventures with him. Or flirting outrageously when he visits. Or texting him way too much if I'm trying to play it cool.

Where he's concerned, I've got about zero chill. I want him, and I don't care if he knows it. At least, I know he really is busy with remodeling and not ghosting me.

After seeing what he's taking on with the remodel, I get why he's so stressed. He still takes the time to grab coffee for his entire demolition crew each morning, fixing each cup the way his people prefer. That's the Martin I've come to know. He thrives on taking care of people, down to the details. He's kind-hearted. It's one reason I trust him despite our brief acquaintance.

My week is going well until Joel and Wes stop in again to complain about Haley's game. And yeah, it wasn't exactly the best session ever, but part of that was Joel antagonizing her on purpose. And part of it is that I don't enjoy playing with the group anymore.

I wish I could continue avoiding the confrontation, but I'm working. I can't exactly bail and leave Paz alone to handle the rest of the morning rush on his own. A fact Joel must have counted on when he decided to strike now. Wes looks reluctant to be there with him, which only makes me dread whatever Joel has to say more. Sure enough, he starts in as soon as he's placed his order for a large coffee with an obscene amount of flavor syrup and espresso shots.

"Come on, Bob, suck it up. Consider the group's best interest. We need a decent DM to run the next campaign," Joel wheedles.

"Sorry, dude, we're swamped. I really can't talk about DMing right now." That's the truth. Joel's visit is during our morning rush. It's not like he can reasonably dispute that I'm too busy to talk. Wes tries to chivy Joel away once they pay, rather than holding up the line to harangue me about DMing, yet again.

Joel still insists on getting in another crack at me. "You're the only one without a legitimate job, man."

Theo and Laura, two of my regulars who like to game, are next in line. And Theo has no filter, so he blurts out his unsolicited advice to Joel. "Speaking as a DM, games suck if the person running them isn't feeling it. And DMing sucks if your group acts like a bunch of unappreciative jerks. Maybe Bob would be more interested in running a game for you if you weren't being a demanding dick about it."

Laura stifles a laugh. "Pretty sure he wasn't asking you, Thee." She nudges his shoulder.

"Yeah, well, if he asked me while being passive aggressive as shit about my job, I'd tell him right where to stick it, but Bob is nicer than me." Theo turns to me and winks. "I'd invite you to our game, if you need a new group, but we play at work, so it's employees only. But, check out Roll20. I've played online some, and it works pretty well. You might even discover a group who appreciates you enough not to harass you at work."

"Seriously?" Joel stamps his foot. Hard to say which he dislikes more, being ignored or getting called out over his behavior. I could let it pass and deal with Joel and Wes another day. But I'm fed up, and I deserve not to be bothered at work. And Martin just walked in the door. I don't want to be a doormat in front of him. I want to show Martin I'm a partner he can be proud of. Between that and the show of solidarity from Laura and Theo, I find the courage to stand up for myself.

"Yeah, seriously." I say. Joel looks startled that I'm not rolling over for him. "I've had enough of your BS, Joel. The only time you visit or contact me at all is to bully me into doing what you want, and I don't want to run a game. Which I already told you. Even if I did, you'd never be satisfied. I'd rather run a campaign that balances fighting with roleplay and puzzles, like Haley, which is half of what you hate about our games recently."

He stares at me, mouth working, but no words coming out. Wes speaks first.

"So, is that a no?" Wes asks.

"Yeah. It's a no." I agree. "And I'm done. I'll be looking for another group, because I don't appreciate the amount of disrespect you guys give me over not having some fancy finance job like you."

"Oh. Sorry, man. I didn't realize it bothered you." Wes looks genuinely apologetic, but come on, how did he not realize calling my job a joke is insulting?

"Of course it bothered me, Wes." I try to keep my irritation out of my tone, with minimal success based on his shamefaced expression.

Paz calls out Joel and Wes's order at the far end of the counter before things can get any more awkward. Wes looks like he actually regrets making me miserable when we play.

"I'm sorry, man. I guess I should have realized we were upsetting you. If you change your mind about playing with us, I'll dial back the shitty comments and I won't keep ragging on you to run our game. You do what's best for you. Come on, Joel." Wes drags Joel over to collect their drinks and they leave.

Joel still looks disgruntled, but Wes has him in hand. I'll still need to text the group chat that I'm officially out of the group, but it boosts my entire mood to have decided to move on from them. I'm ready for something new. And an online platform like Theo suggested would make it easier to find a group I'm compatible with.

"Way to put them in their place, Bob." Theo offers me an elbow bump in solidarity and I oblige. I get his chocolate fix for him, since Paz just set out a fresh batch of brownies and Theo is a sucker for them.

When Martin gets up to the counter to order, he beams at me. "Good morning, Bobby. Did I overhear you taking Joel down a peg?"

"You did." I grin at him. "Same order as yesterday, handsome?"

"Yes. My crew is making the demolition fly. We should get everything fixed by the summer fling, knock on wood." He pays, and I get to work pouring his coffees while we chat.

"That's fantastic. I'm excited to meet your friends and see what the club is like with a crowd." Martin invited me to the party, so I'm not being presumptuous about attending. The more I think about it, the more the party excites me.

"You'll love it. The fling is always an outstanding event, and with it also being the grand reopening this year, I'm sure it will be our biggest one yet."

"Sounds great. I'm glad the plans are on track." I grin at him.

"They are. We're hoping to get everything torn out this week. If that all goes to plan, Harry will start construction next week. That gives him seven more weeks to finish the job in time. I'm getting excited to order all the new fixtures and furniture."

"I'll bet. Let me know if you need volunteers."

"Watch it, I might take you up on that." Martin waggles a finger at me, playfully warning me off. God, his teasing smile does things to me.

"I've got tomorrow off, if you need me to knock down walls."

"No need to give up your day off. I've got a big enough crew coming in. Plus, I'm paying everyone else there for their time, so putting you to work as a volunteer would be wrong. But, since you don't have work in the morning, how would you like to get together again tonight? Tabby has dinner plans with a friend, so I'm free."

"Sounds wonderful. I had an early shift today, so I'll finish work before you. Pick me up at my place around six?" I'm not sure if I want him to mean tonight as a date or another chance to play with all his toys. Both would be perfect. I pour the last cup and fit the eight coffees into a carrier for him.

"Can't wait." Martin agrees. He collects his order, adding cream and sugar to the various cups, and leaves with a last backward glance. I wave after him, feeling all kinds of sappy about seeing him later.

***

True to his word, Martin picks me up after he finishes his work. His hair is still damp from his shower. Is it weird that I'd like to see him all sweaty and dusty from tearing out ruined drywall?

Probably. That doesn't stop me from getting a boner at the mental image of him sweaty from a hard day's work.

Martin texts to ask if I've eaten before coming to get me, then says I shouldn't when I tell him not yet. So either he wants to fuck me silly or he's planning a dinner date. I'm alright with either of those options. Both would be damn near perfect.

We make small talk as we drive. Martin takes me to Adventures rather than a restaurant, so I figure we're just fucking. It shouldn't disappoint me, but it does. At least a little. I've started hoping that I might be more to him than a good time.

We talked about exclusivity and boyfriends, after all. Even if it is a bit fast. Not that we don't have incredible sex. But I want more. After the way he held me following our sex games, I thought there might be deeper feelings taking root on both our parts. That level of caring certainly got my heart all involved. Oh well, I can dial back my expectations for sex this good.

When we get inside, Martin kisses me. "So, hot stuff, you up for a game after I take you out to dinner?"

"Huh?" Talk about emotional whiplash. So, this *is* a proper date. We're going to dinner. He likes me as more than a fling. "What kind of game?" I try to play it cool even though I'm doing a happy dance on the inside.

"I was thinking I could surprise you, if you're still good with what we discussed last time?"

"Yeah. Sounds good," I agree, mind already racing to guess which part of the extensive list of kinks he is referring to.

"Good. Come on, I meant to grab something for you earlier, but I forgot it here." Martin leads me inside. We traipse through the plastic drapes meant to keep the construction debris out of reception. "Sorry for the mess. This should only take a minute."

"It's fine." I look around the space. They've already removed all the furniture that used to be in here and stripped most of the back wall down to the studs. They've also made a solid start of tearing out the old flooring.

I'm curious how it will look upon completion. But not curious enough to linger when Martin beckons me into one of the private rooms. They taped the door off with plastic to keep it clean, so Martin peels that off to let us inside. I follow him into what can only be the room he described as medical themed.

"Let's see if they're where I expect." Martin goes right over to the built-in cabinets and grabs a zipped up black case that reminds me of a shaving kit. His back blocks me from seeing what's inside when he unzips it to check the contents. "Perfect, I think you're in for a treat, Bobby." Martin smiles at me over his shoulder as he closes the case back up and tucks it under his arm.

"Is that all you wanted?" I ask when he turns toward the exit. It's small and doesn't give me any obvious idea of what he has in mind for tonight.

"Why? Would you prefer we stick around to roleplay a little?" Martin gestures at the authentic-looking exam table, taking up pride of place along one wall. It makes the room look like a doctor's office. "I could be your sexy doctor and give you a prostate exam."

"Maybe another time," I say, unsure whether medical roleplay would be as much fun as our game the other night. Might make it hard to look my actual doctor in the eye the next time I need a prostate exam if Martin turns the entire experience into an orgasm-fest. Better not risk it.

"Another time." Martin winks at me. He holds open the door, then reseals the plastic over it before we leave the club with whatever mystery item we came here to retrieve.

If his plan is to drive me wild with anticipation, it more than works. By the time we're seated at our table, I'm consumed with curiosity and my fantasies about whatever he has planned have my dick very interested in the proceedings. For all of that, we have a real conversation about our hopes and dreams as we eat.

Martin doesn't scoff at my interest in working at Sin long-term. Or my management ambitions. He even praises me for sticking to something I want to do, despite social pressures to do something more glamorous. We discuss our interests, and he tells me more about Charlie and Tabitha. It feels like a date. A fantastic date with a man I can talk with for ages.

Martin asks if I'm okay with him ordering for us. When I agree, he gets several tapas dishes for us to share. Which I appreciate, since I went to the trouble of cleaning out before he came over and I'd hate to end the night too full to fuck. Especially with that mystery box looming at the back of my thoughts. What does he have planned?

"You ready to go back to your place, Bobby?" Martin asks when he catches me fidgeting yet again once we've finished most of the food.

"Yeah." I tap my toes against his foot under the table.

"What do you think will happen once we're there?" Martin runs his fingers along my arm.

"I don't know, except that I really hope it includes your dick in my ass." I lower my voice so he's the only one to hear me.

"You want me to fuck you?" Martin leans closer, mirroring my posture and low voice.

"You know I do."

"I do now." He strokes my arm again. "And I'd be more than happy to oblige. You mentioned that someday you'd like to play without condoms, and every time you squirm in your seat, do you know what it makes me want to do to you?"

"What?"

“I want to fuck you full of my cum, plug you up tight, and make you hold my jizz inside while we go to eat before I let you come. Ever since you mentioned wanting that the other night, I’ve been thinking about it.”

That sounds like a delicious promise, and I’m all for it. I bite back my moan of lust. Martin timed his teasing for just before the server returned with the machine to take our payment. So I can’t tell him how hot that idea sounds. That is not playing fair.

Martin makes polite small talk with the server as he pays. He gives me a wicked grin once she leaves. “You like the sound of that?”

“Yes. God, yes. Please tell me that is something we can actually do someday?”

“Some day, my filthy boy.” Martin leans in and kisses my cheek. “Come on, your surprise awaits.”

I follow him out of the booth, walking a little stiffly until I can will my dick to wilt.

CHAPTER 13

Martin

I have Bobby go clean up while I get set up for our fun and games. He nods absently when I ask where he keeps the items I need. He mentioned wanting to try this when we spoke about our kinks, so I am confident he'll enjoy the surprise. Sounds aren't something I've played with much. I called up Doc, the retired physician who donated most of Adventures' medical kink equipment to get the lowdown on safety and risks.

Bob's kitchen is tiny, so it's easy to find a pot to boil water in for sterilizing the surgical steel rods. It takes a while, but I make use of the time to get everything else set up, including the new tube of surgical grade sterile lube I picked up for the occasion.

The noise of the shower running cuts off shortly after I've got the sounds cooled to room temp. Bobby's bed is made with a fresh sheet from his closet. Everything we'll need neatly arrayed on a sterile field that I set up on the side table. Bobby comes out in nothing but a cloud of steam.

"So, what's this surprise?" He saunters toward me. The sight of my naked lover at ease in his own space has me sorely tempted to just skip right to the fucking. From the state of his half hard dick, Bobby would be on board. But I want more than a quick orgasm from him. I want to help him lose himself in new experiences that we can explore together. So I resist the urge to sweep him into a heated embrace that will surely lead to fucking him senseless.

"Sit on the bed and I'll show you." I sweep my hand toward where I want him, and Bobby does as I ask. He sits, letting his knees fall open so I have an unobstructed view of his cock. I want him hard for this. "Jerk yourself. This will be easier with your dick erect."

Bobby bites back a moan and grabs his dick. I watch as he strokes himself. Damn, he's sexy with his head thrown back in pleasure and the glistening head of his cock poking up out of his fist.

"Tell me what you're thinking about while you touch yourself," I ask.

"Thinking about you." Bobby's eyes flutter open, and he watches me, seeking approval. I nod and smile, gesturing for him to go on. His breath catches as he rubs his sensitive glans. "The way you fucked me after our game on Monday. I want you inside me again."

"You'll have me, but first we're trying something new. Stop touching your dick before you come and we have to wait for it to get hard again."

"Yeah? What do you have in mind?" Bobby releases his grip and smoothes his palms over his thighs. Clearly, not touching himself is an effort. But he's doing it for me, his obedience has me almost as hard as he is.

"Do you recognize these?" I hold up the first sound.

"Um." Bobby licks his lips. His gaze darts over to the array of stainless steel rods in various shapes and sizes. "Oh, fuck. Sounds? Are you going to shove that up my dick?"

"If you ask me nicely." I tease.

"Please stuff that into me. The videos make it seem fucking orgasmic. I didn't think I'd actually get to try it. Is it safe?" Bob wriggles closer to the edge of the bed, bouncing as he rattles off questions. He's adorable when he gets excited like this.

"Glad you're so eager to try it." I chuckle. "I wouldn't have suggested it if it wasn't safe. When done correctly. There are risks. Chief among them UTIs if we don't sterilize everything. I sanitized the sounds while you were in the shower and I've got antibacterial swabs for your dick, just to be sure we aren't introducing bacteria where they don't belong. This lube is sterile and brand new for tonight. And we're going to use a metric fuck ton of it and go slow while we figure out how you like it. It may sting a bit when you pee for a few days after, are you alright with that?"

"Yes."

"Good. One last thing: you're going to hold your cum until I take out the sound. It's not like it will do serious damage if you don't, but it's not ideal. Besides, I don't want you to come too soon. I might even make you wait until you're riding my dick after we're done."

"God, yes. Think I could ride you with one of those in me?" Bobby licks his lips. He looks like he'd love nothing more than to have his dick stuffed while I fuck him into the mattress.

I won't deny the idea of working his prostate from both sides is hot. Doc mentioned that if I insert the sound past the base of his dick it can stimulate him, like a more direct version of massaging his perineum. That might prove a bit intense for our first sounding session, and I need to read up on it more before we go there. If he enjoys tonight, I might look at getting him a cage with a cock plug so he can be stuffed full, fore and aft.

Bobby mentioned chastity along with sounding. If he wants to be mine, the idea of controlling his orgasms tangibly appeals to me. That might be getting ahead of myself, but I want to make Bobby mine. My boy to play with, fuss over, and maybe even to love.

Whoa. It's way too soon for that. Mind-blowing sex and the intense high of a scene can make it easy to bond fast, that's all. I'm not ready to call this love, yet. But I can see us going there if we follow this trajectory.

Dinner tonight proved that we can enjoy each other's company outside of sex and kink. I enjoyed talking with him about everything from the club to his game group and what he enjoys about non-sexy role play.

I can't get enough of him. Not just the sex. The way he flirts and jokes with me. The way he entrusts himself in my care. From the first time he fell apart in my arms, I've wanted to be his safe haven.

"Are you ready?" I ask.

"Ready when you are, handsome."

So I disinfect my hands, swab his dick, and apply a generous drizzle of lube over his slit. Then I lightly squeeze the head to open him up, coat the sound in more lube, and slot it into place. Bob gasps at the initial penetration. I go slow, feeding the rod gently into his dick.

"Oh, fuck," he hisses between his teeth, his fingers dig into my thigh.

"Color?" I check, pausing in case he wants me to stop. His straining dick and the expression on his face say he's into it, but best to be sure.

"Green. So fucking green." Bobby arches into the sensation. I stroke his dick, pushing the sound a little deeper as I stimulate him. Bobby's guttural moans of pleasure and the lift of his hips beg me for more. "That's, ugh, so good."

I get the rod in as deep as I want it and give him a few gentle thrusts that have him gasping and pleading.

"Oh, Martin. Fuck, I need to come. Oh, my god. Handsome, fuck, it's so intense. It's, fuck. Please?"

I chuckle at his desperation and give him a few more slow slides of the sound. At the same time, I wrap my other hand around his shaft so that his cock gets stimulation inside and out and it drives him right to the edge.

"It's too much. Let me come, please. Gonna... can't..." he's panting with need.

"Come for me," I demand as I slide the sound out in a smooth glide. Bobby's cum shoots from his dick as I'm withdrawing the sound. He makes the most incredible moans of pleasure, groaning and curling forward as I set aside the sound to stroke him through his orgasm.

I kiss him as hot cum gushes over my hand, and he thrusts helplessly against me. He kisses back, desperate and needy, and when his dick softens, he climbs into my lap and burrows against my chest.

"Thank you, Martin," he whispers. His naked ass grinding against my erection has me thinking all kinds of filthy thoughts. But I just hold him until he recovers enough to sit back and meet my gaze.

"Good?" I ask.

"So good." He nods, then he shimmies his ass against my bulge. "You liked it too."

"I did. Making you come is hot, Bobby boy."

"Mhm. I enjoy making you come, too. I cleaned myself up for you earlier. If you want to fuck me."

"You sure you're up to it right now?"

"Yeah. Want to feel you. Wish we could go bare."

"Not yet, hot stuff. In a couple months, we can get tested and go from there."

Bobby sighs. "I guess that's fair. You're a wonderful boyfriend, always taking care of me. A good dom too." He kisses me again, grinding his ass against me.

"Boyfriend, huh?"

"Yeah. I mean, we agreed to be exclusive with the orgasms, right? So, boyfriend. Unless you want to call it something else?" He worries his lip between his teeth. I gently thumb at his mouth to get him to stop and focus on me.

"Boyfriend is fine. Whatever you like, hot stuff."

"Good. Then in a few months, when we're in the clear for the testing window, you're going to fill me up with your jizz. For now, we can use condoms."

"That we can, bossy." I agree, amused at how forward he can be. I reach for the rubber I set out with the other supplies earlier. Once I've got it on, Bobby straddles my lap, grinding teasingly against me until I give his ass a swat.

"Settle down."

He pouts, but holds still long enough for me to get us situated so I can fuck into him.

After Bobby's shower prep, it doesn't take much to push inside. Once I get my dick lined up with his hole, he lowers himself onto my cock. The sensation of sinking into him is almost as good as watching him come undone. And the fact I'm more excited about coaxing another orgasm out of him than chasing my own, is just more confirmation that Bobby already has me wrapped around his finger. I'm more than happy to call him my boyfriend, or any other title he craves, if it means I get to keep sex with him all to myself.

CHAPTER 14

Bob

After our dinner date, Martin and I text more often. We spent hours chatting over our meal, so it no longer seems intrusive to text him with random thoughts and jokes throughout the day. He's more than a casual sex partner. I've got a boyfriend who cares about more than getting laid.

I send him goodnight selfies, just to be silly. Most mornings, I wake up to a good morning text from him. He sends me updates on the club, and Tabby's various auditions.

And we sext about all the wild fantasies I want to try with him. It's still surreal that he tried sounding with me after I told him it was something I'd been interested in for a while.

Despite his ridiculous schedule this summer, between overseeing things at the club and accompanying Tabby to her auditions all over the continent, Martin makes time for me, too. We play at my place several more times and go out on more dates. And the sex is still incredible, even the times we do it with no toys or games involved. We talk too. About everything.

I'm falling for him. Ever since he pulled me into his arms and told me I was wonderful in the backseat of his car after our first time, I suspected he was worth knowing. I can see a future with Martin. The initial rush of emotion might have owed more to endorphins than true love, but we've built on that foundation with every encounter.

Martin must reciprocate, because if he wasn't serious about us, I doubt he'd have invited me over to his house to meet Tabby. Letting me call him my boyfriend is mere words, introducing me to his kid means he's serious about us. Martin told her he's seeing me after our first official date.

I've even video chatted with her when she and her dad were in New York for more dance auditions last week. I know he'd miss her if she moved to the US, let alone across the continent, but he still supports her dreams. He's a great dad. And tonight is my first official meeting with his kid. I'm anxious to make a good impression.

Martin offered to pick me up, but he's got a ton on his plate and he's cooking our meal, so I told him not to worry about it. When I show up with a bottle of wine to go with our dinner, Tabby is the one who opens the door.

"Hey," Tabby looks me up and down.

"Hi, Tabby, it's nice to meet you." I thrust the bottle of wine toward her. She frowns as she takes it. God, her stern face makes her look like her dad. They have the same dark eyes. Only her glare doesn't have the heat of desire in it that her dad's does when he aims it at me during our play. That's probably a good thing.

"What's this? Are you trying to bribe me into liking you with booze?" Tabby deadpans. Great, is she going to tell her dad I'm trying to corrupt his child? Fuck. I have to make a good impression tonight if I expect this relationship with Martin to continue.

"What? No! Not at all. I just, you know, host gift…" I backpedal, uncertain how offended she really is.

"Relax. I'm old enough to drink," Tabby laughs, her stern expression melting away. "You're too easy. It's nice to meet the guy who's made my dad so smiley lately. He deserves to be happy again." Tabby steps back and gestures for me to come inside.

I do, taking off my shoes and placing them on the rack by the door. "So, you're cool with me dating him?"

"Sure. Why wouldn't I be? My dad hasn't dated anyone seriously since mom died. So, you must be pretty special to him. I'm glad he won't be all alone when I move out." She turns toward the hallway and I follow her, past a wall of family photos chronicling Tabby's life, from infant to prima ballerina.

"Have you heard from the dance companies where you auditioned?" I ask, trying not to study the photos for signs of Charlie. It's not like I'm competing with Tabby's mom or anything.

"Not yet." Tabby shrugs. "They said this week, so we'll see."

"Well, hope you hear soon."

"Thanks," Tabby smiles over her shoulder at me as we step into the kitchen, where her dad is pulling something that smells delicious out of the oven. She sets the wine down on the counter. "I approve of the boyfriend, Dad."

"Oh, wonderful," Martin says dryly. He sets down the food, some sort of saucy, cheesy casserole, from the look of it. "Glad to have your seal of approval. I see Bobby brought along some wine. Want to set out the wine glasses, Tabby Cat?"

"Sure, I live to serve," Tabby drawls, but she goes to the cabinet by the sink to get the glasses.

Martin removes his oven mitts and comes to give me a hug and a peck on the lips. "Hey, hot stuff. Perfect timing."

"Hi," I say back. "Need a hand in here?"

"Everything is finished. If you could open the wine while I bring the food to the table, we can get started." Martin pulls open a drawer to hand me the bottle opener. He takes the casserole dish over to the laden table. Tabby is already dishing salad onto her plate as I wrestle with the cork. When I get the bottle open, I join them both to sit.

“This smells incredible.”

“Dad’s a catch,” Tabby winks at me.

“Garlic makes everything smell delicious,” Martin demurs. “It’s just baked chicken, garlic bread, cheesy potatoes, and salad, nothing fancy.”

“Looks fancier than what I make out of a box,” I joke.

It’s no secret that I’m not the best cook. The one time we ate at my place after he came over for a visit, I burned a frozen pizza all to hell. Warming up deserts at work is about the extent of my culinary skills. I can make a mean latte though, with the foamy art on top and everything. After the pizza debacle, Martin and I have kept to meals out or grabbing takeaway on our dates. Delivery if we’re in an indulgent mood after a hard fuck.

Martin reaches over to pat my hand. “I figured we could enjoy something homey, since we seem to eat out a lot when we get together.”

Conversation revolves around the food for a while as we eat. Tabby asks me questions about what I do and how I met her dad. I reciprocate with questions about her dancing. Midway through the meal, she gets a call. Her eyes light up when she reads the caller ID. “Daddy, I need to take this,” she says, pushing away from the table.

Martin nods, taking a sip of his wine. Tabby turns away from us to answer the call.

“Hello?” She’s already striding away from the table, her back to us as she confirms who she is for the person on the other end of the line. Tabby walks out of the room to talk in private. The hushed tone of her voice through the closed door doesn’t reveal much about the conversation.

Martin reaches for my hand, and I can tell he's nervous for her. I squeeze, hoping to reassure him. It's nice to be the one he can lean on for a change. Just because I love the way he takes care of me during and after our scenes doesn't mean I never want to reciprocate. The chance to support him with my presence is wonderfully fulfilling. It's proof he can depend on me as much as I rely on him.

Tabby shrieks from the other room. Martin gets to his feet. His daughter charges back into the dining area, phone no longer in evidence. She does a leap and a twirl. "I did it! I got offered a junior position at BC Ballet."

Martin sweeps her into a fierce embrace. We both fall all over ourselves to congratulate her.

"I'm still moving out when I start, but it will be nice to be based close to home," Tabby enthuses.

"Can't wait to watch your first performance," I chip in.

"This calls for a celebration!" Martin declares. He and Tabby both sit back in their seats.

"I'm so proud of you, Tabitha. I still remember the first time your mom and I took you to see the ballet."

Tabby rolls her eyes. "I know the story. I begged you both for lessons."

"Your eyes were as wide as saucers as soon as the music started and the first dancer took the stage. I knew right then that you'd found your passion. You spent the first year of lessons crying that you'd never be as good as the older kids." Martin recounts the story with the air of oft repeated family lore. This is an important memory for them and it's sweet. But it makes me feel like an outsider.

"Mom made me stick with it, because 'nothing good ever comes without hard work'." Tabby shakes her head.

"That was one of her favorite quotes. You worked your butt off for this, Tabby." Martin reaches over to pat his daughter's hand.

"Yep. I still remember how you sobbed like a baby when I earned my ballet laces. Thanks for supporting me, Dad."

"Always. Now, let's finish eating before I get any more sappy. Then we can all go for celebratory ice cream." Martin puts his napkin back in his lap and takes another bite of his food.

"I can leave, if you two want to celebrate without me," I offer. The two of them reminiscing makes me ache to be a part of their family and feature in some of their shared memories years from now. Martin has never made me feel like I'm competing with Charlie for a place in his heart, but I want to be a part of this closeness. My relationship with Martin is still new. I don't know if I belong here tonight.

"No, don't leave," Tabby says. "You're important to my dad, so I want to get to know you. Stay and celebrate with us. Dad says you're getting a promotion at work? We can celebrate that and the club's grand reopening, too. We each get a pint at the grocery store, it's a family tradition."

I glance between Tabby and Martin, still uncertain that I belong.

"I'd like you to stay as well. You are welcome here, Bobby. But if you'd rather go, I can take you home," Martin offers.

"I… okay. Guess I'll stay, then." I swallow hard.

Tabby inviting me into their family traditions to celebrate her big news is overwhelming in the best way. She really is accepting me as her dad's partner. Not just paying lip service. In however many years, when they tell the story of the day she got offered her first dance contract, I'll be a part of the memory.

I can only hope I'll still be with Martin, part of his family. Asking me to stay and be a part of their tradition must mean Martin is really serious about me. He's said as much. His actions, making time for me with everything else going on in his life, back up that assertion. But hearing it from her makes it more real.

Martin and his daughter are both willing to invite me into their family. It's a good thing I still have plenty of wine in my glass. I'm choked up at being included. Hiding my face behind a sip of my drink is the best I can manage not to embarrass myself by tearing up in front of them. Martin's the first guy I've dated who I can see myself calling family.

"Good." Martin smiles at me, his foot caresses mine under the table. The look in his eyes says he knows how deeply their acceptance matters to me. He turns the conversation away from anything heavy. "So, which flavor of ice cream are you thinking of getting?"

"Blueberry cheesecake, duh," Tabby says. "What about you, Bob?"

"Um, Tiger Tail."

"Ew, licorice. Really?" Tabby makes a face at me.

"Tabby," Martin says in a warning tone.

"I mean, it's cool. Sorry. You like what you like. I never got why they wouldn't make the swirls chocolate. That way it would still resemble a tiger, but the flavor would have broader appeal."

"I like the way it tastes." I shrug. Few people I know seem to agree with me, but that only means more ice cream for me. "What about you, Martin?"

"Dad's boring, he always gets vanilla." Tabby rolls her eyes at him. I've been reading up on the kinky lingo, so I snort, stifling a laugh now that I get why it's funny that he likes vanilla so much. In his ice coffee, and apparently his ice cream.

"I like the classics," Martin shrugs off his daughter's scorn for his ice cream preferences. Guess I'm in good company, since she doesn't like mine either.

We finish our meal with Tabby eagerly making plans for once she signs the official contract. I help them put away the leftovers. After that, we walk to the store to pick out our pints and eat them on the couch, right out of the container.

By the end of the night, I'm more comfortable with my place in their home. Tabby teases us about being sappy in love when her dad kisses me through a mouthful of vanilla ice cream. Later that night, Tabby leaves to go tell her friends her good news.

With his daughter out of the house, the things Martin does to me in his bed with the rest of that vanilla ice cream are decidedly not vanilla. His sheets bear the brunt of our temperature play. I end up sleeping over after a warm soak in his tub while he puts on fresh ones. Drifting off in his arms, I hope there are a lot more nights like this in our future.

CHAPTER 15

Martin

Adventures's annual Summer Fling is in full swing all around me. Harry pulled through with getting the entire renovation completed in our two-month timeframe. The work is impeccable. He transformed the damaged, all-purpose space that I've made do with since the club opened, into my dream public play area. Complete with a separate lounge for club members to relax and chat.

The work just wrapped up last week. This is the big reveal of the renovations for most of my members and the positive response is overwhelming. It's worth the utter chaos of cleaning and setting everything up for the party in time once the work crews left.

Tonight would have been special regardless, but it's even more important because it's my chance to introduce Bobby to everyone who matters in my life. Other than Tabby.

The two of them get along wonderfully. She enjoys teasing him and keeping him on his toes. But tonight is about showing Bobby my community and my friends. I want this to be a place where he can belong and meet others who relate to the things we're exploring together.

From the folks who work for me, in reception and as dungeon monitors, to the various members who gather here. I've missed having the main room open during the remodel. Adventures is more than a kink club, it's my second home and a safe space to be themselves for the people who gather here.

It doesn't take long for Bobby to garner interest as a new member. Especially since he sticks to my side like a burr at first. It's rare for me to partner up at the club for more than a scene. So it draws attention that he doesn't leave my side, other than to get us both drinks.

Tate and Monty are the first of the little sub collective who are among my most loyal club members to pounce on him. They approach arm in arm.

"Hi, Martin," Monty speaks first, bouncing up on his toes like he's not sure he should ask whatever question is on the tip of his tongue. With Monty, you never can tell. He has terrible impulse control. "Is it true?"

"Is what true, Monty?"

"That this is your new boy? Quent said you told Kylee he is." Monty gestures at Bob.

"It's true." I nod. "This is my boyfriend and sub, Bob. Bobby, these two lovely boys are Monty and Tate."

"Hi," Monty waves. "Nice to meet you, Bob. Are you a little? Tate and I are."

"Um, I don't think so? I'm still new to the whole kink thing."

"That's okay, Martin's a great dom. I'm sure you'll learn a lot playing with him. He gives wonderful spankings."

"Oh. You've played with him?" Bobby asks. I hold my breath, wondering if he'll get upset or jealous. We've talked about scening with other people. He's met some of my friends while we were setting up for tonight, but this is the first time I have exposed him to public play.

"A few times, nothing serious, though. I'm mostly looking for a daddy dom to spank me and make me behave. And I like age play, which Martin isn't into, right, Sir?" Monty bats his eyes at me.

"That's right, Monty." I give Bobby's hand a reassuring squeeze, but he doesn't seem to need it. He smiles at Monty.

"He does give a good spanking." Bobby beams at me, his smile speaking volumes. He wriggles in his seat, like he's remembering our most recent scene before we had to buckle down and get the club ready for tonight. He's certainly taken to that aspect of our play, among others. I'm sure the plug in his ass is going to have him wild with lust by the time we go home tonight.

"Guess the search for my perfect daddy continues." Monty sighs dramatically.

"You know exactly who you want to be your daddy, and it isn't Martin." Tate cuts his eyes toward where Luke is examining the new hardpoints we had installed on a solid steel frame above the upgraded event stage for suspension work.

Monty follows Tate's gaze, then notices what Luke is doing. His gleeful shriek draws a few eyes, but he hardly seems to care. Monty grabs my arm.

"Oh my god, Martin! Sir, is that what I think it is?" Monty bounces on his toes and acts the part of a sugared up toddler told he can have cake.

"It is. Harry went all out on the materials and we consulted with Luke on the load limits to be sure it's safe."

"So, Daddy Luke can make me fly in front of the entire club? You're the best! I can't wait to try it. I need to go ask him if he'll play with me before he's booked up for months." Monty starts toward the stage, then turns back toward me and Bob. "Thank you for adding that, Sir. It was nice to meet you, Bob." He ends the conversation as politely as I've ever heard him. Sure, his cheerful goodbyes are an afterthought, but even that is an improvement in his manners over the last time we played. Before the pipe burst.

"He's been playing with a daddy all summer, but since the club was closed, he's trying to be all coy about who it is." Tate informs me when he catches me watching Monty jog up to Luke.

"Ah." I turn my attention back to Bobby and Tate.

"He thinks I don't notice the way he looks at my brother. The two of them are nowhere near as subtle as they think they are. Anyway, if you both want, I could introduce Bob to the rest of the Adventurers' crew?"

"Adventurers' crew?" Bobby glances between Tate and me for an explanation.

"It's a group of subs who meet every Tuesday at Adventures," I say. "They're the ones I told you about who game here before we officially open some nights."

Tate nods and takes up the explanation. "And we meet up most weekends. There are four of us regulars, plus Quent convinced Harry to run a D&D campaign for us when he was building a kennel for them and Mistress Kylee. We do littles nights twice a month since most of us are littles or pups. And we go out together, outside of kink events, too. The movies, the beach, shopping, game nights, you name it and we've probably done it."

"Game nights?" Bob perks up at that. He still hasn't found the right fit since leaving his regular gaming group. I mentioned the club has a group that meets, but he worried about getting in over his head when he was still testing the waters with the lifestyle. Considering everything we've explored this summer, he has nothing to worry about. The boy took to being my sub like a duck to water.

"Yep, like I said, Harry runs a D&D game once a month and the rest of the time it's board games and stuff. Would you want to play with us? Our party doesn't have a healer at the moment, so we could use a fifth player."

"That would be amazing. I just left my old group earlier this summer," Bobby admits.

"Cool, well, everyone except Harry is here tonight. He usually skips the kinky stuff."

Bobby hesitates, still uncertain of his footing and whether he needs to demur to me for permission while we're at the club. That's not our style. I'm mostly his dom when we scene and his boyfriend outside of that. It's a setup that suits us both well. It's no surprise that he's reticent, since he's never been to a party quite like this before. Still, in the hour since the doors have opened, he's relaxed considerably, acting more like his usual bold self, and I can tell he's interested in Tate's offer.

I know Tate will look out for him amongst the crowd. Besides, I don't tolerate bullies. If anyone wants to play at Adventures, they damn well better have consent before they start anything on my turf. No one should bother Bobby, even if he isn't at my side. Not unless he wants to be bothered. The flip side to that is as long as they follow club rules and all parties are into it, pretty much anything goes, within reason.

"Go on and meet the others, hot stuff." I nudge him.

"Yeah, I think I will." Bobby leans in to kiss me, then follows Tate into the crowd, only the slightest hitch in his step to betray the hardware in his pants.

I stay at our table, surveying my dream fulfilled. My club, exactly as Charlie and I had always imagined it, full of people getting to be themselves. The fact I get to share it with a new partner makes tonight even more sweet.

Bobby and I have plans for later. Just thinking about him with his cock caged and plugged and his ass stuffed with a vibrating plug has me longing for our private after party.

Our test results came back negative. So to celebrate, we're going to live out his fantasy of fucking bareback. Knowing him, there will be roleplay involved, since he's been missing the less kinky version lately. Hopefully, he'll hit it off with the Adventurers crew so he can finally scratch the itch that initially brought us together.

It's strange to consider that if Bob hadn't been searching for his perfect dungeon master at just the right time, we might not be here. Exactly where I want to be with my hot stuff. In love and in my dungeon.

***

Thanks for reading! If you're looking for more Summer of Adventures be sure to pre-order the next novella in this series, Knotty Boy at www.amzn.com/B09D4NG4L7

Sin and Chocolate is a cafe that first appeared in my Table Topped series and Bob makes several appearances. Theo, Paz and Laura each have their own stories, so be sure to check out Table Topped at https://www.amazon.com/gp/product/B08R6LM6YG

And if you want more kink, check out New Ground, an M/M/X urban fantasy novel with psychic links and daddy kink. www.amzn.com/B08NHQFJDZ

ABOUT THE AUTHOR

Alex Silver (he/them) grew up mostly in Northern Maine and is now living in Canada with one spouse, two kids, and three birds. Alex is a trans guy who started writing fiction as a child and never stopped. Although there were detours through assisting on a farm and being a pharmacist along the way.

Visit me online at:

http://alexsilverauthor.wordpress.com/

Join my Facebook group at:

https://www.facebook.com/groups/alexsalcove

Follow me on BookBub at:

https://www.bookbub.com/profile/alex-silver

Sign up for my newsletter for a free short story at: https://landing.mailerlite.com/webforms/landing/i2w6l7

And as always, consider leaving a review on Amazon or Goodreads if you enjoyed this book, reviews are of vital importance to independent authors, thanks!

Be sure to explore my entire catalog at Amazon:

SUMMER OF ADVENTURES

Kinky Contemporary Romance

Dungeon Master (M/M) Book 1
www.amzn.com/B09D9ZTWDK
Knotty Boy (M/M) Book 2
www.amzn.com/B09D4NG4L7
Service Call (M/M) Book 3
www.amzn.com/B09YDNFJ5V
Picture Perfect (M/X) Book 4
www.amzn.com/B09YDN81N7
Puppy Love (F/X) Book 5
www.amzn.com/B09YFBWCKV
Stud Muffin (M/M/M) Book 6
www.amzn.com/B0B51XVMGX

TABLE TOPPED

Roll for Initiative (M/M) Book 1

www.amzn.com/B08R6M1XBT

Charisma Check (M/M) Book 2

www.amzn.com/B08R6J14VZ

Saving Throw (M/NB) Book 3

www.amzn.com/B08SL3WF2Q

Plus One Bonus (M/X) Book 4

www.amzn.com/B091V3G8DL

Dump Stat (F/F) Book 5

www.amzn.com/B0992TD65Y

HAUNTASTIC HAUNTS SERIES

Dan's Hauntastic Haunts Investigates: Goodman Dairy (*Book 1)* www.amzn.com/B07YSV2ZNQ
Dan's Hauntastic Haunts Investigates: Hawk Lake (*Book 2)* www.amzn.com/B081LM3WXP
Dan's Hauntastic Haunts Investigates: Ivarsson School (*Book 3*) www.amzn.com/B087QPR6TD

Drew's Haunted Hangout (*A Hauntastic Haunts Short Story 1)*
Rafael's Haunted Halloween (*A Hauntastic Haunts Short Story 2)*
Lee's Haunted Holiday (*A Hauntastic Haunts Short Story 3*)

PSIONS OF SPIRE SERIES

Shelter	Novella 0.5	www.amzn.com/B07NM9XL8K
Bright Spark	Book 1	www.amzn.com/B07NZ8KPS6
Bold Move	Novella 1.5	www.amzn.com/B07YVGZXDM
Keen Sense	Book 2	www.amzn.com/B07R6L8W91
Weak Link	Novella 2.5	www.amzn.com/B07T4J2LJZ
Quick Fire	Book 3	www.amzn.com/B07VGTF3NB
Clear Sight	Book 4	www.amzn.com/B07ZQP7BDS
New Look	Book 4.5	www.amzn.com/B08F4GBK63
New Ground	A SPIREverse daddy kink standalone	www.amzn.com/B08NHQFJDZ

Manufactured by Amazon.ca
Bolton, ON